Lost in Las Vegas

A Frost & Crowe Mystery

Kristen Painter

Lost in Las Vegas
A Frost & Crowe Mystery

Copyright © 2020 Kristen Painter

This book is a work of fiction. The characters, events, and places portrayed in this book are products of the author's imagination and are either fictitious or are used fictitiously. Any similarity to real person, living or dead, is purely coincidental and not intended by the author.

Lost in Las Vegas

In this new Jayne Frost and Sinclair Crowe mystery, a royal road trip takes the Princess and Prince Consort of the North Pole all the way to Las Vegas.

And even though they're in Sin City on official business, it doesn't take long for trouble to find them. Trouble that's very close to home. In fact, Sinclair's entire family is gambling on him and Jayne figuring out what's gone dangerously wrong with the cool new magic trick at the end of his parents' show.

Thankfully, they have help from a few friends and a pair of talking cats. But how many times can they roll the dice before time runs out?

Chapter One

Sinclair

Was there a more beautiful woman in the world than my Jayne?

Not possible. At least not to me. Over my second cup of coffee, I watched her as she got another helping of blueberry pancakes from the breakfast buffet set up by palace staff.

She still had that half-awake thing going on where her hair was a little rumpled and her eyes were only half-opened, but it charmed me to no end. And while I would have been fine still being in bed with her, starting the day with her parents had become our new routine.

I didn't mind it. I didn't mind any of this new life. I loved it, actually.

Marrying her was the best thing I'd ever done. Of course, it might also be argued that my decision to move to Nocturne Falls and open up a doughnut shop could actually be the best thing I'd ever done because that's what led to meeting her. Either way, Jayne was definitely the most incredible person I'd ever known. Beautiful, talented, funny, sweet, and mine.

Not to diminish my parents in any way. My parents were great people. Wonderful, loving, supportive. Everything you could want in a mother and father. Just like Jayne's parents were everything I could have hoped for as in-laws. They'd welcomed me in with such love and warmth that I'd never for one moment felt like I wasn't a part of the family.

I guess I just never imagined married life would be so cool. Not to make a winter elf pun or anything, seeing as how that's what she was. She was also heir to the Winter Throne, which could not be overlooked since it made her an actual princess.

Technically, marrying her had made me royal too. Prince Consort. That was my title. Me, a necromancer, actual royalty. Sure, it was by marriage, but still. How crazy was that? Even more amazing was that Jack Frost, her father and the Winter King, had made a special decree giving my parents the titles of Lord and Lady.

If that wasn't a gracious gesture, then such things didn't exist. I don't believe my mother has ever been so tickled by anything in her life. But then if marriage could make a necromancer into a Prince Consort, it wasn't much of a stretch that a royal decree could make a zombie into a Lady. Lady Lila Crowe. It did have a nice ring to it.

I sipped my coffee, watching as Jayne poured blueberry syrup over those blueberry pancakes. A lot of syrup. So Jayne. If a little was good, a lot was better. Death and ruin, I loved that woman. There was no way not to smile.

About everything, really.

Life in the palace was incredibly good. Our new apartment within the palace had been finished while we'd been on our three-week honeymoon (one week on an Alaskan cruise, one week in Vegas with my folks, then a week in Hawaii) and the place was great.

We wanted for nothing. Part of being royalty, I suppose. No one would expect to live in a palace and be miserable. At least not because of lack of creature comforts. Even our cats, Spider and Sugar, had a big, brand-new, custom cat condo for them to lounge around on and look out the windows.

But despite all that goodness, I'd be lying if I said I wasn't a little bored. I hated to even think that way. To even let that word enter my brain. It felt wrong. Like I wasn't appreciating all the wonderful stuff around me. But life felt a little too easy. And maybe, if I was really being honest, part of me felt like I was getting away with something. Like I didn't quite deserve all this luxury and poshness that I'd fallen into.

Many times I'd mulled the idea of opening up a new doughnut shop. It would be great to get my hands in dough again and put the old brain to work on creating new flavor combinations. But I wasn't sure how that idea would fly. Royals lived by a different set of standards.

They didn't seem to work unless it was directly related to running the kingdom or some kind of charitable pursuit. Now, of course, in the case of Jayne's uncle, things were different. He definitely worked.

But then he was Santa Claus. Toys and all that were his business. I supposed if I did something adjacent to that aspect of things, it would be okay. His wife, Martha, was making a name for herself with her eggnog fudge now that it was being sold in the Santa's Workshop Toy Stores. But how did I make doughnuts work with toys?

It didn't really compute.

So as much as I would have loved having another doughnut shop, I didn't want to rock the boat either. Not with how wonderful things were. I was not going to be the fly in the ointment, so to speak. But I knew I was going to have to find something to keep my brain more active. I needed the daily challenge the doughnut shop had provided.

And I had to figure out how to get that challenge without letting Jayne know what was going on. Not yet, anyway. I twisted my wedding ring around my finger.

I hated that she might think I didn't like it here because that wasn't the truth. I loved the North Pole. It was the most magical place I'd ever lived. Second only to Las Vegas, which was a very different kind of magic. Okay and third to Nocturne Falls, also a very different kind of magic.

Maybe what it all boiled down to was that I just wasn't used to working so little to get so much. It felt unbalanced. Which led me back to feeling not quite deserving and a touch guilty. Clearly, I had some issues to deal with.

But how did I deal with them without making everyone else around me suffer? Maybe I should call my dad. He was a great sounding board and had never steered me wrong. Same thing with my mom, really. She was more of a listener and a soother, which I loved, but my dad was always happy to make suggestions. Usually very good ones.

Jayne came back with her plate, smiling at me. "You look pensive."

I smiled back. "Just trying to decide if I should have a second apple-cranberry turnover."

She leaned in and kissed me. "You definitely should. They're one of the kitchen's best pastries." She took her seat, flicking her napkin out over her lap. "But that's not really what you were thinking about, was it?"

Did she know me that well? "I might have had a few other things on my mind."

She cut a bite of pancake, delicately stabbing her fork into it. She yawned and blinked a few times. "Like what?"

I leaned in. "Like how adorable you are before you're fully awake."

She laughed. "Sure."

I pretended to be aghast. "You don't believe me?"

She ate her pancakes. "I just know that look, and it means there's something else going on in your head."

I shrugged. "I think you're confusing it with my I-need-another-cup-of-coffee look." I picked up my cup and got to my feet. "Be right back."

Her father seemed to have the same idea, meeting me at the urn. I let him go first. He was the king, after all.

He gave me a nod of thanks. "Do you have much planned for the day?"

I took a breath before answering, choosing my words carefully but being honest. "Not as much as I'd like."

He nodded again, like he understood. "You'll find a rhythm."

As he moved his full cup out of the way, I put mine under the spigot. "I hope so." The second that sentence left my mouth, I realized how ungrateful it sounded. "I mean, I'm sure I will."

Jack eyed me with the kind of searching gaze I'd seen in Jayne on several occasions. His voice was low and plainly meant to keep this conversation between us. "I know this is a very different life than what you're used to."

I smiled, maybe bigger than necessary. "It is, but I love it."

Jack smiled in return. "You love Jayne."

"I do."

"The rest will come. You'll see." He left me to fix my coffee and to think about what he'd said. Did he know what I was struggling with? Or was he just good at guessing? I had no idea.

I could only be thankful he was so understanding. The last thing I wanted was to upset the father of my bride.

And not just because he was the king of my new homeland.

Chapter Two

Jayne

Seeing my dad and my husband talk like old friends made my heart happy. Well, happier. I was already pretty much on Cloud Nine. I was a newlywed, after all. If you couldn't be blissful as a newlywed, there was something wrong with you. Just saying.

And being married to Sin was so much more than I'd ever imagined could happen to me. He was the best guy ever. Sweet and handsome and so smart, loved cats, loved *me*, was kind and generous, had incredible parents, could talk to the dead, and had no problems with my constant need for sugar and Dr Pepper.

Also, so hot. Like next-level hot.

The man was a keeper. And I had no plans on ever letting him go. Ever. Did I say ever? Because I meant it.

Which was why I had to figure out what was bothering him. Call it a wife's intuition, but something wasn't quite right with my guy. And that bothered me. I wanted him to be as happy as I was. Or at least as happy as a necromancer could be.

It couldn't be me that was causing him to get all introspective. We were too much in love with each other for him to be upset at something I'd done. Besides, we hadn't done much of anything lately. Except for, you know, husband and wife kind of stuff.

That made me smile again.

So if it wasn't me, what was it? Could he be missing his folks? We'd had such a great visit with them. Tons of fun, lots of great meals, plenty of laughter and a little sightseeing for me since I'd never been to Vegas before. Maybe our visit had made him realize how much he missed spending time with them.

For a second, I wondered if I should invite them up again, but I knew they were getting ready to debut a new finale trick in their Las Vegas show, *Dead Sexy*. There was no way they'd take a break from rehearsing to come for a visit. I wasn't even sure they could. I knew they stuck to a pretty rigid schedule.

And really, it wouldn't be right of me to expect them to drop everything. Their show was a mega-hit on the Strip. I'd seen it for myself on our weeklong visit there.

Hands down, the coolest, craziest live performance I'd ever seen. Not that I'd seen a lot of live Vegas shows. Or any. But that didn't detract from how jaw-droppingly wild it was with its combination of amazing magic with a little *Walking Dead* flavor and some mystical vibes thrown in. And that was with my full knowledge that Sin's dad, Anson, was a gifted conjurer, and his mom, Lila, was an actual zombie.

Imagine what it must seem like to the regular Joe off the street who didn't know the main performers were supernaturals. No wonder they packed the house every night.

But that was just more reason why asking them to put everything on hold was basically impossible. They couldn't walk away from the show.

Which brought me back to Sin. What was troubling him? He obviously didn't want to tell me. Or at least it wasn't something he was interested in discussing with my parents in earshot.

I knew I should let it go, but... I couldn't. The love of my life was upset about something. It wasn't in me to ignore that.

I worried that pushing him to talk might only upset him more. He'd come to me when he was ready, right? I had to believe that.

He returned with a fresh cup of coffee and took his spot next to me.

My mom was spreading pink grapefruit marmalade on her toast. "Sinclair, would you like to tour the new ribbon factory with me today?"

He looked at her. "I, uh—"

"I was kind of hoping he'd help me in the apartment today, Mom." I knew touring the ribbon factory wasn't going to be high on his list of things to do, although it was kind of my mom to include him. "We really need to get our closet organized."

"It's true," Sin said. "Jayne's stuff keeps creeping onto my side."

My mom laughed. "She'll have the whole thing if you don't watch it. Yes, you'd better work on that. Wait." She stopped laughing. "I thought you each had a closet in that new apartment?"

"We do," Sin answered. "Jayne has one and I have one that Jayne shares with me."

My father snorted. "Sounds about right."

My mother gave him a look before answering. "Well, Sinclair, don't worry about it. You can see the ribbon factory anytime."

He sent me a grateful glance before responding. "I certainly appreciate you including me in that, though."

"Of course." She went back to her toast and the About Town section of the *Pole Post*, the North Pole's newspaper.

Under the table, Sin gave my leg a little squeeze. "Have I told you how much I love you?"

I grinned at him. "Not in the last five minutes."

My mom looked up from the newspaper, smiled, then went back to reading about who'd been seen where.

Sin nodded at the pancakes left on my plate. "Finish those and we'll get to work on that closet."

I harpooned a fluffy triangle of blueberry goodness. "Maybe you could move all your stuff to the linen closet."

He laughed. "You'd like that, wouldn't you?"

I nodded as I chewed. "You only ever wear black jeans, a black or gray T-shirt and your leather jacket."

"Not true," he said, crossing his arms over his gray T-shirt. "I also sometimes wear a white T-shirt. Or black turtlenecks or sweaters."

"Ah, yes." I held my fork up for added punctuation. "Your sweater collection. Of three sweaters. Why did you need your own closet again?"

He laughed, and across from me, my dad shook his head. He looked at my mom. "Like mother, like daughter." He lifted his cup in Sin's direction. "Give them an inch, and they'll take a mile."

Sin winked at me. "It's a good thing she's cute."

I wrinkled my nose. "Hey, I'm more than cute."

"Yes, you are."

I finished my last bite, wiped the syrup off my face with my napkin, then set it on the table beside my plate. "All right. Let's go work on that closet." I nodded at my parents. "See you guys later."

"Have a good day, honey," my mom said.

"You, too."

My father gave us a nod over the top of the sports section. He was sponsoring a crawler team this year, exhibition only, but that didn't stop him from checking the finishing times against the other competitors. Crawlers were the snowmobile-car hybrid vehicles we used to get around in the North Pole.

As we walked out the door and down the hall, Sin slipped his hand in mine. "You know I wouldn't have minded visiting the ribbon factory with your mom."

"I know. But I also know it's not the kind of thing that's high on your list of exciting ways to spend your day."

"True." He stared straight ahead, brows slightly bent as his pensive look returned.

Was he thinking about what really excited him? Was that it? Did life in the NP lack that certain something he'd had in Nocturne Falls?

To be honest, if that's what he was feeling, I totally got it. Life in the North Pole was great. But it wasn't like our life in Nocturne Falls at all. Life there had been something new every day.

Here it was much more about routine, especially now that the wedding and Christmas were both behind us. We pretty much knew on a daily basis what was coming. That was never true about life in Nocturne Falls. Not for long, anyway.

Was I on to something? Or just projecting? I couldn't be sure without talking to him, and I didn't want to put him on the spot. If he was a little bored, I could guarantee he wouldn't want me to know. He'd think it would hurt my feelings.

Truth was, there were times when I was a little bored. Maybe more than a little. But growing up royal, you learned to fill your downtime with things like reading and charity work and writing letters.

But for a guy like Sin, how fulfilling could that be? I wasn't sure.

He'd given up a lot to move here with me. His business, his friends, even his beloved muscle car.

I hugged his arm, feeling suddenly responsible for him in a way I hadn't before.

Something had to be done.

Chapter Three

Sinclair

About an hour into organizing our closet, which mostly consisted of me watching from the chair in our bedroom while Jayne tried to decide which of her fifty black dresses were keepers and which ones could be donated, the doorbell rang.

Spider, who'd been lying on the bed with Sugar, suddenly lifted his head. "Door, Mama."

Jayne stuck herself halfway out of the closet as she was pulling on another dress. "I heard it."

He stood up, looking very proud of himself. "Treats for Spider."

Sugar came alive too. "Treats?"

Jayne laughed. "No, neither of you get treats for telling me someone's at the door when I already heard there was someone at the door."

Chuckling, I got to my feet. "I'll get it." I walked

out of the room, still shaking my head. If you'd told me I'd someday be royalty, living with two talking cats in the North Pole in a palace, I would have told you that you were nuts. And yet, here I was.

I opened the door to find a footman with an envelope on a silver tray. He gave a short bow, something else I didn't think I'd ever get used to. "For you and Princess Frost, sir."

"Thank you." I took the note and shut the door as the footman retreated. "Jayne?"

"Yes," she called back.

"We got a message."

"What's it say?"

I returned to the bedroom, opening the ivory envelope as I walked. "Not sure yet."

She came out of the closet in yet another little black dress, looking as phenomenal as she had in the last ten.

I took the card from the envelope and read. "Jayne and Sinclair, please come to my office at your earliest convenience. Jack."

Frowning slightly, I looked at her. "Why would your father send us a note instead of just calling?"

"Because he knew if he called, I'd ask him what the meeting is about, and he obviously doesn't want to say until we get there." She made a face. "It must be something one of us, or both of us, isn't going to like. Or he thinks we won't like. He wants to have his say before we start with questions."

16

I blinked hard, trying to guess what Jack might want us for.

She crossed her arms and leaned against the closet door. "I already don't like it."

I laughed, despite my concern. "Sweetheart, you don't know what it is."

"Yes, but I know my father. Whatever he's up to, he thinks we are going to be against it, but we probably won't be able to say no."

My curiosity and unease were building with similar speed. "What could it be?"

She shook her head slowly. "I have no idea. Which makes me even more suspicious." She tapped her finger against her bottom lip. "Maybe I should call my mother, but he's probably got her locked down too. Or she doesn't know anything about it. Which is probably more likely because she's not great at keeping secrets."

"Plus, she's off at the ribbon factory, so he might have waited until she left to even have this meeting. If he's trying to keep it a secret."

"True," Jayne said.

I set the note and envelope on the desk. I didn't want to put this off for another second. "We should go to his office and see what this is all about then. It does say at our earliest convenience."

"True." She leaned for a second longer before righting herself. "All right. Let's see what he's got up his sleeve. Well, as soon as I change. I don't want him thinking I dressed up for this conversation."

She was definitely more at ease with this than I was. Had we done something wrong? Worse, had I done something wrong? Broken some royal protocol?

I hoped not. I'd taken classes on how to be a royal before we were married, and I liked to think I'd gotten a decent handle on it. I certainly didn't want to screw up and cause my new family embarrassment.

But then Jayne hadn't said anything, and surely, she would have noticed if I'd made a mistake big enough to warrant a meeting.

I snorted softly. I was worrying for nothing. At least that's what I told myself.

After Jayne changed, we left the apartment and walked to Jack's office in silence. Jayne went in ahead of me.

"Morning, Mrs. Greenbaum. My dad wanted to see us."

"Morning, Princess Jayne. Morning, Prince Consort Sinclair." Mrs. Greenbaum, Jack's administrative assistant, tucked one last file away in its proper spot, closed the filing cabinet drawer, then went to her desk and put her hand on the phone. "Would you like me to let him know you're here?"

Jayne nodded. "Sure."

Normally, Jayne would have gone right in. I'd seen her do it before. Maybe she was a little nervous after all.

18

Mrs. Greenbaum picked up the phone. "Your highness, Princess Jayne and Prince Consort Sinclair are here." She listened, nodding. "Very good, sir."

She hung up. "Go right on in." She gave Jayne a knowing look. "There are scones on the conference table."

"Lingonberry?" Jayne asked.

I knew for a fact Mrs. Greenbaum's lingonberry scones were one of Jayne's favorite things. They were exceptionally delicious. If I'd still had my shop, I would have been working on a way to duplicate the flavors in a doughnut.

"Of course," Mrs. Greenbaum said. "Is there any other kind?"

"Nope." Jayne walked into her father's office with more confidence than I was feeling.

I liked Jack Frost a lot. As a ruler, he seemed generous and fair. As a father-in-law, he'd been gracious and welcoming. But that didn't mean he wasn't still a little intimidating.

Especially when the man had an enormous slab of glacier as his desktop. The magic it took to keep that from melting away was staggering. It was a pretty bold way of reminding everyone who entered his office what he was capable of and that he was very much the Winter King.

But then I got the sense that he wasn't as powerful and successful as he was by accident.

It was another great reminder that my bride

was his heir apparent and wielded a hefty amount of magic herself, even if it wasn't on such obvious display.

"Hi, Dad," Jayne said. "You wanted to see us?"

He looked up from some paperwork as we came in. Thankfully, he smiled. "That was fast. I just sent the note."

Jayne laughed as she went over to the conference table across from his desk and took a scone from the plate there. "You said at our earliest convenience. So here we are." She looked at me. "Sin, you want a scone?"

"No, thanks." My appetite was on hold until I knew more. Jayne's appetite rarely took such a break, which was just another one of her superpowers.

"True," Jack said. "I did say your earliest. I just didn't think you'd come until your closet was finished. Thanks for coming so quickly. Have a seat."

We sat. Jayne bit the corner off her scone.

"How is the closet coming?"

Jayne shrugged. "It's coming." She slouched a little, concentrating on the pastry in her hand and clearly pretending she wasn't anxious to know why we'd been summoned. "You could have called if that's all you wanted to know."

He smiled at her, then looked at me. "Just like her mother. You have your hands full with this one."

"Yes, sir," I answered. "I'm aware."

Jack interlaced his fingers on top of the

paperwork he'd just been reading. "I'm sure you're wondering what's going on."

I nodded. "Yes, sir."

Jayne snorted. "Dad, why else do you think we're here? Spill it."

Jack hesitated as if he was choosing his words. Or perhaps deciding where to start. "Your wedding was arguably the biggest event we've had in the North Pole in some time. The turnout was staggering. People are still talking about it. All of that got Kris and I to thinking."

Santa had been thinking about us. I wasn't sure if that was good or bad.

"We've decided to send you out on a tour of the stores. Strictly as a morale booster. A meet and greet opportunity. Initially only the highest-grossing stores will make the short list for a visit, however, we're giving the rest of the stores the chance to bring their sales up to qualify. We think it could increase sales by as much as twenty percent in some regions. And as we're on the downside of Christmas, that could be something."

I almost exhaled in relief. Visiting stores wasn't something I'd considered, but it also wasn't something terrible. Actually, it might be interesting. I'd only ever seen the one in Nocturne Falls where Jayne was working when we met.

Jayne sat up straight, gesturing with the remaining scone. "Hold on. You want us to kiss hands and shake babies, all in the name of sales?"

I leaned over. "It's shake hands and kiss babies."

She shot me a look. "You do things your way. I'll do things mine." Her gaze returned to her father. "Dad, seriously?"

"Jayne, this is a royal obligation. You're the Princess and Prince Consort. You're beloved figures who represent the North Pole. It's time to put that popularity to good use."

She frowned. "For real?"

I was already warming to the idea. For one thing, I liked travel. For another, none of the toy stores the company owned were in the North Pole. It would be a real break from royal life. "I think it sounds interesting."

Jack smiled at me. "It should be. We have stores all over the world. Although at first we'll concentrate on those in the continental US."

Jayne looked at me. "You think it sounds interesting?"

"Sure. Seeing new places. Meeting new people. Putting my royal title to good use." I wasn't so convinced about the royal part yet, because the fact that people might want to meet me simply for the reason that I'd married into the royal family seemed crazy, but I knew royalty could have that effect on some. "What's not to like about those things?"

She stared at me a second longer, a happy gleam coming into her eyes. Then she looked at her dad.

"Tell us more. How long would we be gone? Do we get a sleigh for travel? I'm not going without Spider or Sugar. Which store would we start with? When would we have to leave?"

Jack laughed and held up his hands. "One question at a time. Here's what your uncle and I have been thinking…"

Chapter Four

Jayne

My dad took a breath. "We know Sinclair's parents are launching their new finale trick in two weeks, so we thought we'd start with the Las Vegas location. It's not our top-grossing store, but it does do very well, and that would allow you both a chance to see Sinclair's parents and have another visit with them while also being there in time to see the new illusion. So long as that would work for them."

"I'm sure they'd make it work." Sin smiled for the first time since we'd entered my dad's office. "That's very kind of you to think of them."

My dad shrugged, looking pleased with himself. "To be honest, we all talked about coming down."

"All?" I asked.

"Your mom and me, plus your aunt and uncle." He smiled at Sin. "We really enjoyed getting to know your parents while they were here, and we'd love to see their show. Unfortunately, it's just not going to work with our schedules."

Sin nodded. "They would love to have you any time you can make it." His smile faded a touch. "Two weeks. That means we'd be leaving soon then."

My dad nodded. "Yes. The plan would be for you to leave in the next few days. To answer Jayne's question of how you'd travel, we've arranged an RV for you. Ezreal assures me it's the nicest one money can buy. Say, Sinclair, can you drive a vehicle that large? I hope you can because the coach was custom-fitted."

"I can. Wait, do I need a CDL?"

"No, no special license. But if you're not comfortable with being behind the wheel of something that size, we can hire a driver for you. We just thought the RV would allow you to bring the cats and travel in more comfort since it wouldn't require you to move in and out of hotels."

"I love it," Sin said. "And I have no problem driving a big vehicle like that. How long is it?"

"Forty-five feet."

Sin's brows shot up. "Wow."

"Hold up." I brushed scone crumbs off my lap. "An RV?"

"I promise it's nice," my dad said. "Do you think your uncle and I would set you up in anything less than the best? And do you think, with the unlimited budget we gave Ezreal, that he'd arrange for anything that wasn't top-notch?"

"No, but it's still a *camper*, right?" The images in my mind were taking me to some very cramped quarters. Could you even stand upright in a camper? And wasn't the shower like a twelve by twelve square that required you to stand on the toilet? I was starting to have minor palpitations. I didn't think of myself as spoiled, but I wasn't exactly the kind of girl who like the simplicity of camping either.

I traveled with a tiara, for snowball's sake.

Sin shook his head. "I don't think what your father is talking about would qualify as a camper."

"Sinclair's right. This is more of a tour bus than a pop-up pull behind. It has all the comforts of home. Actually, it's built on a bus frame."

"All the comforts of home?" I crossed my arms and sat back. "So it has a hot tub?"

"Well, no, but that sort of thing will probably be available at whatever RV park you set up at." My father looked at Sinclair like he was hoping for a lifeline. "I would imagine, anyway."

"This sounds like fun," Sin said. "So we'd pick up the RV where?"

"Anchorage. It's the closest portal. Of course, that's why you'd have to leave soon. It's roughly an eight-day drive from there to Las Vegas."

I went a little stiff. "Eight days?"

Sinclair grinned. "I bet the drive from Anchorage to Vegas is amazing."

I stared at him. "Eight days?" That sounded like torture. Eight days in an RV? I couldn't picture a vehicle nice enough that I'd want to spend eight days in it. Or even two, honestly.

"Imagine all the country we'd see. And I'll do the driving. I'd enjoy it, actually."

My father looked so pleased with himself. "You're a good man, Sinclair."

"I don't know." I glanced at Sin again. He looked so happy. Like this was the best thing that had happened to him since we got married. "Couldn't we just fly?"

"You could," my father answered. "But then the cats would have to travel in the cargo hold and—"

"No." I put my hand down hard on his desk, the cold immediately seeping into my palm. "I'm not doing that to them."

"Well, this way they could roam around and have their space."

I did like that part. And how happy Sin looked. Was this what he needed? A new adventure? For him, I could endure anything. Even being cramped into a camper. At least we'd be together. And have the cats with us. I'd focus on that while I was standing on the toilet trying to wash my hair. "Okay, I'm in."

My father's grin went wide. "Excellent. Ezreal will accompany you to Anchorage and make sure you're all set with the RV. You have two days to pack. Make sure you take your bracelet in case you need to hide your identity. I realize blue hair isn't that odd of a sight these days, but your ears still give you away as an elf."

"Bracelet?" Sin asked.

My father nodded. "For winter elves who travel outside of the realm, we have magical bracelets that can hide our true looks. They basically hide our ears and the color of our hair."

"Nice," Sin said.

I blinked at both of them, just chatting like this was any other conversation. "Hang on. I don't even know how long to pack for."

"I'd say at least a month. Maybe two."

"Are you kidding?" Son of a nutcracker, that was a long time to live like a sardine.

"Well, we'd like you to visit quite a few stores. We'll have the rest of the itinerary figured out by the time you reach Vegas, I'm sure. Or at least before you leave. And we may add more stops as you go so best to be prepared."

Prepared. For a month or two of living in a camper going who knows where to smile and wave and be our royal selves.

My dad had lost his mind.

Sin shook his hand. "We'll do the kingdom proud."

"I know you will," my dad said.

We walked straight back to our apartment. I was lost in thought. So much so that it took me a second to realize Sin had said something. "What was that?"

"I just said how amazing this trip is going to be."

I frowned. "You really think so?"

"Sure, why wouldn't it be?"

"I just... I don't know. We were just kind of getting settled into life here."

He opened the door to our apartment and let me in first, following behind. When the door was shut, he spoke again. "Our life here is great, don't get me wrong, but it's not the most...engaging life."

My heart sank a little. "I knew it. You're bored. Oh, honey, I'm so sorry. Why didn't you say anything?"

"I didn't want to make you feel bad. I love you, and I love my new life. It's just not as..."

"Challenging?"

He nodded. "I miss running my own business and coming up with new ideas and feeling like I was accomplishing something. I'm sorry. I'm sure in time that would change. But right now I don't feel as useful as I'd like."

I wrapped my arms around him. "You know what? I totally get it. Becoming a royal is a big adjustment. And not one any class can truly prepare you for." I wanted to change all of that for him. And I realized how important this royal tour might be. Not to mention how it was happening at just the right time.

Had my dad sensed Sinclair was getting restless?

Sin hugged me back, kissing the top of my head. "I would never want to cause a problem for you."

I leaned away to see his face. "I know you wouldn't. But I love you, and you're my husband, and your happiness is very important to me. And that is never something I'd consider a problem." I smiled with everything I had in me. "We need to start packing."

New light sparkled in his eyes. "You're sure you want to do this trip?"

"I've never wanted to do anything more in my life. Outside of marrying you, which I already did."

"Trip, Mama?" Spider sat a few feet away.

Sugar wasn't too far behind him. She sat up and pawed the air. It was something new she'd just started doing. "Trip, Momlady?"

And that was her new name for me. Momlady. Cats were so funny. Talking cats, even more so.

Sin let me go to answer the cats. "Yep. Looks like we're all going on a new adventure. Better pick out your favorite toys."

At the word toy, Sugar perked up. "Mouses?"

"Sure," Sin said. "Bring all the mouses you want." He looked at me, grabbing my hand. "I promise I'll be the best Prince Consort you could possibly imagine. I will kiss every hand and shake every baby you put in front of me."

"You're already the best Prince Consort I could

possibly imagine. And it will be great to see your folks again." I was starting to get excited about this. A little.

"They will be so thrilled we're coming back. I'd better call them and let them know." He didn't let go of my hand though. And he hadn't stopped smiling.

"You really love a road trip, huh?"

"Who doesn't?" He tugged me close again. "There is nothing better than getting to see the country while also being in control of your journey. If you want to stop to see the world's largest ball of tin foil, you can. If you want to stop at a roadside stand and buy homemade jam, you can. If you want to take a detour, you can do that too. Your day is up to you. I'm sure we'll have some sort of schedule to keep to, but there has to be free time built in."

I squinted at him. "Are you making that up?"

"About the free time?"

"About the world's largest ball of tin foil."

"No, it really exists. Haven't you ever been on a road trip?"

I shook my head. "Not really. I mean, I've been on sleigh trips, but you know how fast that thing travels."

He picked me up and whirled me around, making me laugh. "Oh man, Jayne, you are in for a great time."

When he put me down and I caught my breath, I tipped my head and tried not to look too skeptical.

"If you say so. Although I do really want to see that ball of tin foil now."

He chuckled. "As your driver and tour guide, I will do my best to make it happen. Now let's get those suitcases down and get packing."

Easy for him to say. Even easier for him to do. Planning for a trip that required me to be Princess Jayne in an official capacity took a little more doing.

Good thing we'd just about squared that closet away. I took a deep breath and headed in.

Chapter Five

Sinclair

I didn't know if Jack was a mind reader or he'd sensed my mood or it was all just serendipity, but I'd never been more pumped about a trip in my life. Okay, our honeymoon was amazing. It really was.

But this was a road trip. In what I *knew* was going to be a killer RV. And I was getting to drive.

I had a feeling that Jayne's reluctance, which was about as easy to see as her pretty pointed ears, would disappear in a hot second once we got underway.

And if it didn't, I'd do everything in my power to help her see just how much fun a road trip could be. I'd stop at every diner, roadside stand, cheesy attraction, scenic overlook and point of interest along the way if it made her happy. Giant balls of tin foil, houses made from beer cans, enormous dinosaur statues…we'd see it all.

I'd enjoy it too. There was something special about seeing the country at your own pace. Finding all the hidden gems along the way. I'd driven cross-country a few times on my own. But this trip, with her at my side, was bound to be epic.

Packing was a real undertaking. It took the better part of our two days. In part because there was some clothing that had to be cleaned and pressed but also in part because we were packing for a more involved excursion. Even our honeymoon hadn't required this level of wardrobe.

We also hadn't taken the cats with us on the honeymoon. Ezreal had assured us the RV would be equipped with the necessities they needed, like food bowls, litter box, and a scratching post, but that we should bring anything that might help them feel at home in their new surroundings.

According to Spider and Sugar, this meant toys, treats, their favorite brush, Sugar's pink blanket that Aunt Birdie had crocheted for her and Spider's boo mouse, which was actually a catnip-stuffed ghost he'd gotten last Halloween.

As for us, well, I'd never gone on a road trip that required taking suits before, but considering that we were representing the kingdom, I understood. At least we were only doing meet and greets and not full-blown royal functions, like dinners.

Those were a little tedious, if I'm being honest. Usually there was someone interesting to talk to but not always. And on those occasions, being a royal felt like a tremendous amount of work.

I hoped this wasn't like that. But if it was, I'd suck it up and keep a smile on my face. After all, I'd married Jayne knowing full well what I was getting into.

"I think I'm done." She stood back from her second suitcase, gazing into it like the secrets of the universe were contained inside. And maybe they were. She certainly had everything else in there. "I just need to get the appropriate jewels from Davide and I'm good to go."

"What jewels do you need?" I was sure the RV had decent security, but I didn't love the idea of traveling with the kind of sparklers she typically wore to royal functions.

"My traveling set." She looked at me. "This is a state secret, by the way, but I have an exact replica of my snowflake tiara done in cubic zirconia. I have a pair of diamond earrings, a diamond bracelet and a House of Frost sapphire and diamond crest done the same way."

"Really? That's genius." And a big relief.

She nodded. "My mom has the same thing. It just takes the risk out of losing the real ones. Or having them swiped, which has never happened yet, thankfully."

"And thankfully, it won't be attempted either."

"Right." She went to the phone and dialed.

"Davide? Hi. Yes. You heard? Okay, great. Yes, for him too. Sure, I'm here. Thanks." She hung up.

I wiggled my finger at her. "What's that 'for him too' business?"

Her look said I might not like her answer and she didn't care. "You're the Prince Consort. Did you think you weren't getting some sparkly things too?"

I shot a look right back at her. "Like what?"

"Like a good watch and a House of Frost lapel pin."

"What's a good watch?"

"The same kind my father wears. A Patek Philippe. Although yours won't have as many diamonds."

"Well, then, that's fine." I almost laughed. If all I had to do to look princely was wear a flashy fake watch and a lapel pin, I was good with it.

Davide showed up a few minutes later with a simple black case. It had a fingerprint lock, which he programmed to open using either of our index fingers, and then we were done.

When he left, I looked at Jayne. "Should we call for the footmen then?"

She looked around, a little bit of longing in her gaze. "I guess so. I can't believe we're leaving this brand-new apartment. We've barely moved in."

"We'll be back."

"I know." She still didn't look happy.

"Hey," I said softly. "Home is where we make

36

it. And with Spider and Sugar with us, what else do we need?"

She nodded. "You're right, I know. I just…" She shrugged. "I feel a little melancholy, that's all."

"You're allowed."

Spider and Sugar came tearing through, jumped on the bed, then back off the bed and out again.

She laughed. "They'd better get that out of their system. There won't be room for that nonsense on the camper."

I laughed. "Honey, it is not a camper. I promise."

"You haven't seen it."

"Yeah, but I have a pretty good idea of what a forty-five-foot RV is going to look like." I gave her side a little tickle, then grinned my most lecherous grin. "Just think. You're going to be trapped with me."

She laughed. "You'll be driving. Hard for you to do much from behind the wheel."

I stalked closer, still leering. "But when we stop…"

She shrieked and tried to dodge past me, but I caught her. "I have to call the footmen!"

I nuzzled her neck. "The footmen can wait."

And wait they did. An hour later, after our recreational activities, they arrived to haul all our stuff down to the South exit, where Ezreal and a large crawler awaited us.

So did Jayne's parents and aunt and uncle, all

there to say goodbye and wish us well. Jayne's aunt also had a container of eggnog fudge for us, something Jayne immediately took possession of.

We said goodbye with lots of hugs and handshakes, then I helped Jayne get situated in the back seat with the cats in their carriers. As she kept them occupied, Ezreal and I got the rest of the luggage loaded, a job we easily handled ourselves. It wasn't that I didn't trust the footmen—they were great guys—but there weren't going to be any footmen on the road.

Something I was totally okay with.

Ezreal drove us to the portal, which was about an hour outside of town. The magical doors existed in several locations, but this one was the most used. It opened into Anchorage, Alaska, which wasn't exactly the most convenient of locations, but it was a lot easier to walk into Anchorage wearing a parka than it was Miami. Although, as far as I knew, there wasn't a portal in Miami, either.

The crawler had to stay on the North Pole side, however, so we each took some luggage and carried it through.

Jayne took a cat carrier in each hand, while Ezreal and I dealt with the heavy stuff.

I stared into the back of the crawler. "We're going to have to make two trips."

Ezreal nodded. "Good thing I parked the RV close by."

I couldn't wait to see it, but I tried to keep my excitement on an even keel.

We followed him through, coming out in an empty alleyway. There was snow on the ground, but blue sky peeked through the clouds overhead. Temperature felt about the same.

I hadn't lived in the North Pole that long, but I could sense we'd entered the human world again. Don't ask me how, but the difference was palpable. The energy just wasn't the same. That's the best I could do to describe it.

"This way," Ezreal said.

Jayne went behind him, then I came along, rolling the two suitcases.

We turned a corner and came onto a deserted street. Whether that was because of magical reasons or the town just wasn't busy, I couldn't be sure. The RV was parked across from us. It was enormous, and the navy-blue metallic paint and tinted black windows glittered in the winter sun.

"Son of a nutcracker," Jayne whispered. "Is that the RV?"

"It is," Ezreal said. "Custom Prevost Motor-coach."

My mouth was open, and I didn't care. The beast parked in front of us was deserving of a little awe. I found my voice again. "Good choice, Ezreal."

He turned to grin at me. "Wait until you see the inside."

I was itching to. "Let's get Jayne set up and then we'll get the rest of the stuff."

"Very good." He set down one of the bags he was carrying to dig a key fob out of his pocket. He pressed it. The lights flickered on in the big rig, then he tossed the fob to me. "Here you go."

I caught it and tucked it in my pocket before taking hold of the luggage handles again.

"Is there more than one key?" Jayne asked.

"There's not actually a key," Ezreal answered. "You'll see. Come on."

He led us to the door of the coach, which was how this beautiful piece of machinery really should be referred to. Calling something this impressive an RV seemed like a disservice. He pressed his hand to a pad by the door that looked like it also had a camera in it. A second later, with a soft exhale of air, the door opened, welcoming us aboard.

"Okay," Jayne said. "That's cool."

"Princess," Ezreal said with a smile. "You haven't seen anything yet."

Chapter Six

Jayne

I set the two cat carriers down. I felt like an idiot for all the bad thoughts I'd had about this vehicle. "This is stunning. I can't believe it. I take back everything I ever thought or said about this camper."

The interior looked more like a fancy modern apartment than a motorhome. The floor was white marble tiles veined with black, the cabinets were all high-gloss white, and the trims were in black and deep blue with touches of aqua and natural wood. Wherever there was fabric, like on the couches or the captains' chairs in the front, it was all textured navy leather.

The backsplash in the kitchen was done in a mix of glass tiles in all shades of blue and marble tiles that matched the floor.

"RV." Sinclair and Ezreal said the word at the

exact same time, making me hold my hands up in surrender.

I laughed. "Okay, RV."

"Actually," Sin said, "a vehicle this nice should be called a coach."

Ezreal nodded as he positioned our bags off to one side of the living area. "The Prince Consort is right. This is definitely a motor coach. As you can see, we're in the living-room area, and this behind me is your kitchen."

"I love the little booth." I could see us sitting there, having breakfast.

Ezreal patted the tabletop. "This folds down, and the booth turns into a bed, actually. Not that you'll probably need it with the master bedroom in the back, but it's good to know you have it."

"Yep," I said. "Good to know."

"So you like it?" Sin asked.

"I love everything I can see." The whole thing was gorgeous. And it felt like a home. A very chic, upscale home that a Hollywood celebrity might live in. I had no idea a camper could be this fancy. RV. Coach. Whatever.

Ezreal gestured behind him. "The bedroom and bathroom are in the back. There's a litter box for the cats in the bathroom as well."

I couldn't wait to see that space. The human part, anyway.

He pointed past Sin. "The main entertainment

center is there, but there's another television in the bedroom and one in an exterior compartment designed for use outside. There's also a grill and two camp chairs, all in their own compartments. I'll show you how to open and close the awnings as well."

"Is there satellite?" Sin asked.

"Yes," Ezreal answered. "On the move, satellite will provide your television and internet services. There's also a backup snow globe in the bedroom just in case."

Magical snow globes had been our main form of communication before Ingvar and his tech team had gotten us up and running with sturdier landlines.

"Your uncle even designed a small Santa's Bag for the coach. It's in one of the master bedroom closets. Just in case you need something from home in a hurry."

One of the master bedroom closets? Suddenly, I was a lot more excited about this trip than I had been. "Let's get the rest of our stuff. I'm eager to get the cats settled and get unpacked."

"Speaking of the cats…" He pushed on a narrow panel that ran floor to ceiling. It popped out, then he turned it around and pushed on it again, locking it into place.

On the other side was an attached scratching post with three platforms set at intervals that I knew the cats would be all over. I smiled. "You did a great job with this coach, Ezreal."

He beamed as he came past me. "Thank you, Princess. I hope you and the Prince Consort and the cats are very comfortable."

Sin started down the steps. "We'll be right back, Jayne."

"I'll let the cats out in the bedroom."

"Okay."

As he and Ezreal left to get the rest of our things, I picked the carriers up and took them into the back.

The bedroom actually had a king-size bed. I put the carriers on it, then looked around for a way to shut the door. There was a button on the side of the wall so I pushed it. The door slid closed, *Star Trek*-style. "Are you kidding me? That is so cool." I couldn't have the cats escaping after I set them free.

Spider was already pawing at the carrier's grate. "Mama, Spider wants out."

"Out," Sugar repeated. "Out, Momlady."

"I know you want out, and I'm going to let you, but first, listen to me." I made sure they were both looking at me. Still not a guarantee they were listening, but you took what you could get with cats. "We're in a very big vehicle now. It's a motor coach. And for the next few weeks, we're going to live on this motor coach. You cannot leave the motor coach for any reason or Sinclair and I will be upset. You could get hurt or lost, and that would make us very sad. Do you understand?"

"No leaving. Mama mad."

"Right." Close enough. I looked at Sugar. "You got it?"

She blinked her pretty eyes at me. "Sugar stay put."

"Very good. For now, I'm going to let you out but only in the bedroom so you can explore in here while we get settled, all right? After we're on the road, you can go anywhere you like on the coach."

"Yes, Mama. Hurry."

I opened his carrier first, then Sugar's. They both popped out instantly but then stopped to sniff the air.

"There's supposed to be a litter box in the bathroom," I told them. "I guess we should have a look."

I went through the etched glass door on the other side of the bed. And stopped. I'd been incredibly wrong about imagining having to stand on the toilet to shower. "Snowballs."

The bathroom was remarkable. Obviously not as big as the one in our apartment but just as nicely appointed. Two cobalt-blue glass vessel sinks and a big walk-in shower with lots of white marble tile and plenty of storage space. No tub, but then that seemed like a silly thing to have on what was essentially a land yacht.

I went back out to the bedroom to check that out some more. The top of the mattress was elevated so that it sloped, which would be great for reading or watching TV, but that would have to be flattened out for sleeping. I just didn't know how to do that yet.

Two good-size wardrobes flanked the television opposite the bed, along with plenty of drawers underneath. I was surprised by how much storage there was. One of the wardrobes even had a small safe. The other had the Santa's Bag.

Spider's voice carried from the other room. "Mama Mama Mama."

I went back into the bathroom. "What is it, Spider?"

"Look, Mama. Litter box."

He was standing in it, his head peeking out of the opening. The box had been cleverly hidden in a cabinet beside the toilet. Sugar sat on top of the toilet, watching him.

Thankfully, the lid was down. Starting the trip with a toilet-water-soaked cat didn't seem like the best way to kick things off.

"I'm so glad you found it." I opened the narrow cabinet next to it and found all the supplies necessary to maintain the litter box. Ezreal really had thought of everything.

"All right, you two enjoy your exploring. I'm going back out to help."

Sugar jumped off the toilet seat and zoomed past me to hop up on the bed. "Momlady, window?"

Windows were a big deal for cats. "Oh, right. Let me see." There was a small window on either side of the headboard, which had reading lights built in. A nice touch. I opened the blinds and pulled them up and out of the way. If there was anything these two loved, it was looking outside. "There you go."

Sugar perched herself on the sill that doubled as a nightstand, instantly glued to that little slice of Anchorage. I went to the other side and opened those blinds as well.

I'd been a tiny bit concerned about how the cats were going to do in such a small space and how they'd handle the travel. I was starting to think I'd been worried about nothing. Also, it wasn't that small of a space.

Spider came out of the bathroom and took up residence in the other window a few seconds later.

"You guys good?"

Neither one looked at me.

Spider made a little *eek eek eek* noise at something beyond the glass. "Bird, Mama."

"Good thing you spotted him." I tried not to laugh. "Better keep an eye on him."

Sin and Ezreal were just returning as I left the bedroom, making sure to hit the button to slide the door shut. "You got it all?"

"Yes." Sin set the rest of the bags down, then moved out of the way to let Ezreal add his to the pile.

He hooked a thumb toward the door. "If you want to come outside, I'll give you the rundown of everything out there, then I can go over a few more things inside and that'll be it."

Sin rubbed his hands together, clearly as excited as could be. "Let's do it."

We followed Ezreal as he gave us the grand tour. Not going to lie, it was a little overwhelming, but Sin seemed to have a decent grasp of most of it already. The coach was very impressive. Every available space had been turned into useful storage. There was even a big empty compartment on one side for our luggage when we'd unpacked.

And pretty much everything was as techie as possible. Not only was that a camera at the front door, but it was connected to a monitor in the back that would allow us to see and record anyone who came to our door.

Additionally, there was a tablet that controlled just about everything, from the climate to the slide-outs, whatever those were, to the awnings that would provide us shade when we were parked in a campsite.

I loved that the double awnings were trimmed with LED lights. I could already imagine sitting underneath them with Sin some evening, maybe having our dinner outside, listening to the sounds of nature and taking in the night air.

Was that camping? I couldn't believe I was genuinely looking forward to camping. Maybe marriage was changing me.

Back inside, Ezreal showed us the tablet. He took it out of a pocket behind the driver's seat and turned it on. "This is basically your control panel for everything." He tapped a few buttons.

Things began to move. I grabbed Sin's arm. "Whoa. This gets bigger?"

He smiled. "These are the slide-outs Ezreal mentioned. Only for when we're parked, though."

Ezreal showed me the tablet's screen. "See? Here's where you control those. Just look at the tabs and you should be able to find what you need. Everything outside can be controlled with this too. Not just the awnings but everything out there."

When the slide-outs stopped sliding, I took a walk through. The coach had almost doubled in size. I peeked into the bedroom. It had grown, too.

Spider and Sugar were curled up on the bed together, sleeping. Apparently, travel was exhausting.

I closed the door and went back to Sin and Ezreal. "This is great. I never thought I'd say this, but I love it."

Ezreal made a short bow. "I am very happy to hear you say that, Princess."

He pointed out a few final things to us, one of which was how to flatten the bed, then we said our goodbyes and Sin and I were on our own.

Sin put his hands on his hips and stared at the luggage. "We certainly packed enough."

"And now we have to unpack it."

He sighed, glancing toward the cockpit.

"You want to get on the road, don't you?"

"We do have eight days of travel before we reach Vegas. How are the cats, by the way?"

"They're doing great. Sleeping, actually." An idea came to me. "Why don't you get us underway while I work on the unpacking?"

His brows rose. "You're sure?"

"Sure."

He grinned before leaning in to kiss me. "Buckle up. I mean, metaphorically."

I laughed. "Aye, aye, Captain."

And just like that, our adventure had begun.

Chapter Seven

Sinclair

Jayne's about-face at seeing the coach was everything I'd hoped for and more. It was important to me that she liked the coach, which I figured she would after she'd seen it, but she really seemed to fall in love with it. I was thrilled.

I also couldn't blame her. It was the most amazing RV I'd ever seen. I couldn't imagine what it had cost the kingdom, but I supposed Jack wasn't about to send the heir to his throne out in anything less than the best.

It also told me that his timing had nothing to do with my recent boredom. A custom coach like this didn't happen overnight. This vehicle had been in production for a while. Possibly since before we'd been married.

But then, he'd said the popularity of our wedding had been the impetus for all this. That the event had been what had gotten him and Kris thinking. So maybe they had just paid extra to get the vehicle done quickly.

I didn't really know, but whatever the reason, I was immensely grateful. Not to mention pretty psyched to get behind the wheel.

As expected, it handled beautifully.

Jayne came up to the front. "I'm going to give you the wardrobe and drawers on the right side, and I'll take the ones on the left, if that's okay with you. Which means your side has the Santa's Bag and mine has the safe. Cool?"

"Sounds good. Are you unpacking my stuff?"

"I am. Unless you don't want me to."

"No, that's very sweet of you. Thanks, babe."

Grinning, she leaned in and kissed my cheek. "You *are* doing the driving. I figured it was the least I could do."

"Well, I appreciate it. When we stop next, we'll put the suitcases in that empty compartment outside that Ezreal showed us."

"Perfect. That'll help with space."

Spider slipped past her to stand between the two captain's chairs. He faced her and put a paw on her leg. "Mama, up."

She leaned down and scooped him into her arms. "I thought you were sleeping."

He tucked his head into the crook of her neck. "Sugar snores."

She snorted softly. "Well, you married her."

"Spider loves Sugar." He pushed his head against her chin. "Spider loves Mama too."

She laughed. "And I love you. Why don't you sit up here with Sinclair? You don't mind, do you, honey?"

"Not as long as he just sits there and doesn't climb up onto the dashboard or get under my feet." I glanced over at the little black cat. "Will you be a good boy, Spider?"

"Spider always good."

He was pretty well-behaved. "All right, you can be my navigator."

Jayne put him into the captain's chair beside me. "All right, I'm going back to unpacking."

Spider sat up very straight and stared big-eyed out at the road. "Spider high up."

"Yep, you sit very high up in a motor coach."

"What's motor coach?"

"This vehicle we're in."

"Mama said RV."

"Well, you can call it that too. Both names are correct." I glanced at him. He was clearly fascinated by the view. Spider had been given the gift of gab by a wayward, wish-granting imp that Jayne had accidentally set free from its box.

Spider was initially reluctant to talk around anyone but Jayne, but since Sugar had been gifted her translation collar, he'd gotten chatty around more people.

"What's the navigator?"

"It's the person who helps the driver make sure they're on the right road. The navigator charts the proper route." I wasn't sure what words he understood and what words he didn't, but I figured he'd ask if something stumped him. My cat, on the other hand, whose vocal abilities were produced by a special elf-constructed collar she wore, seemed to mostly focus on treats and doing whatever Spider was doing.

"Route?"

"The path that takes us to where we're going."

"Where's that?"

"We're going to Las Vegas. That's where my parents live."

"Lost Vegas have snow? Spider tired of snow."

"Las Vegas," I corrected him. I knew how he was feeling just a bit. Again, I loved the North Pole, but it was all snow all the time. "And they do get snow, but I don't think they have any right now. Las Vegas is more desert. Lots of sun. And lots of sand."

He seemed to think about that for a moment. "Sounds like litter box."

"It's *not* a litter box." I glanced over at him, and I could swear he was smiling.

He flicked his tail once, turned around, and lay down. "Spider navigator."

It was going to be hard for him to navigate while he was sleeping, but since I doubted his ability to speak parlayed into any kind of map-reading skill, it wasn't like I was counting on him to tell me which exit to take next.

Didn't matter. The trip down through Canada was pretty much a straight shot, and the coach had an excellent satnav in the dash. There was no chance we'd get lost. Well. No chance *I'd* get lost. I knew people who could still manage it, even with help.

I caught glimpses of Jayne, but about an hour later, she came back to the front. "I've got everything put away. You'll probably want to rearrange some stuff, but the suitcases are empty. Guess what else I discovered?"

"What?"

"Ezreal stocked the kitchen for us. At least enough that we could manage a day or two. Wasn't that nice of him?"

"Very nice. He's a great guy. Any chance there's something to drink?"

"Sure." She laughed. "Plenty of Dr Pepper."

I smiled. "I'll take one. They're definitely growing on me."

Our days fell into an easy rhythm. Me behind the wheel, Jayne in the passenger's seat, often with one or both of the cats on her lap or nearby. We made one stop for groceries, ate a few meals at interesting places along the way, bought some maple candies, tried doughnuts at Tim Hortons (good but not as good as mine), and made numerous stops for gas. The miles just disappeared under our wheels.

We talked and laughed, and I fell in love with her all over again. She told me a hundred times how much fun she was having. I think it actually surprised her that the trip was so enjoyable.

Nights we'd put the awnings down, turn on the LED lights, set up our chairs outside and enjoy the evening, even if it was a little cold. The novelty and fun of it all was impossible to ignore, despite the weather.

Jayne didn't mind the cold, of course. Winter elves and cold went together like necromancers and death, but I wasn't as hardy.

At the campsites that had firepits, we took full advantage. We even roasted marshmallows. Sometimes, we'd watch a movie on the pull-out TV. One night, the campers in the spot next to us invited us over to play cards. Jayne was pretty careful to keep her hair down to hide her ears, and it seemed to be working pretty well.

I couldn't think of a time I'd been happier.

I looked over at Jayne, sitting beside me in the slightly warmer climes of Salt Lake City. We'd parked for the night at the KOA campground just outside of town. Our spot had a tree, a little patch of grass and a fire ring, where I had gotten a decent blaze going with some firewood purchased at the camp store. "Tomorrow we reach Vegas."

She nodded. "It'll be great to see your folks again. Are we going to stay in the guest house or the RV?"

I hadn't thought about it, actually. We'd stayed in my parents' guest house when we'd visited on our honeymoon. Guest house made it sound small, but the house was bigger than our new apartment. "Up to you."

She shrugged, a little smile on her face. "The guest house is gorgeous, but we're so settled in here."

"Then let's just park it on the property and call it done. We won't have to move the cats, either."

"You say Spider's name?" Sugar asked.

I glanced over my shoulder. Spider and Sugar were looking at us through the screen door. Despite the cool air, we often left it open so they didn't feel too left out. "No."

Spider stood up on his back legs and put his front paws on the screen. "We come out now."

Jayne turned around. "You guys can't come out here and—" She lowered her voice. "You're not supposed to be talking."

Spider sat down again. He yawned, then licked Sugar on the head a few times. I could have sworn I heard him mutter "Mean" under his breath.

I just shook my head as I faced the fire again. "Is it just me, or are they talking more than usual?"

"I think they're excited by the adventure." She

reached over and took my hand. "And I have to say I completely understand. This has been so much fun. I never thought I'd say that about driving for thirteen hours a day, but spending time with you, even just talking, has been wonderful."

"I couldn't agree more. I'm so glad you're enjoying it. I was worried you'd hate it. You seemed like your mind was already made up in the North Pole."

"You're right, it was a little bit." She stared at the fire. "I didn't know what to expect. It certainly wasn't that hotel suite on wheels behind us."

"It's the most beautiful RV I've ever seen."

"Do you mind driving all those hours? I should be taking a turn, shouldn't I?"

"I don't mind driving at all. I enjoy it, really. But if you want to, I'm happy to let you have a crack at it."

"I'd want to practice first."

A breeze swept through the campsite, making Jayne take her hand back to tug her thick cardigan closer. The fire whipped sideways.

"Are you cold?" I was. "We should go in."

She shrugged. "Just felt a little chill. I think I'm ready to crash."

I stood. "I'll put the fire out and meet you inside." I offered her my hand.

She took it, letting me tug her into my arms. "Don't be long. I need warming up."

"Not to worry, Princess." I knew very well she didn't really need warming up. Didn't matter. I could play along. I kissed the tip of her nose while I slid my hands down to her hips to pull her closer. "You're about to be very warm indeed."

Chapter Eight

Jayne

I woke up to the delicious smells of coffee and pancakes. Sin was in the kitchen, humming something. He sounded very happy.

That made me very happy. I grinned and snuggled deeper into the covers. The RV's bed was incredibly comfortable, and I was perfectly content wrapped in the warm covers. Not to mention Spider was curled up on my pillow beside my head and Sugar was somewhere near my hip. The cats were clearly content as well.

From my cocoon, I called out, "Are you bringing me breakfast in bed?"

"Would you like breakfast in bed?"

I could hear the smile in his voice. "Only if it comes with the chef."

He laughed. "I'll talk to management and see what I can do."

A few minutes later, he came in with a cup of coffee and plate of pancakes, heavily doused with butter and syrup, just the way I liked them.

I sat up a little. "You really are the world's best husband."

He nodded with deep self-satisfaction. "I really am, aren't I?" He bowed. "Your breakfast, madam."

I tugged the covers up, playfully covering myself. "My husband will be back at any moment so don't try anything funny."

Sin laughed. "I hear he's an incredibly handsome man with a terrible temper, so I'll be on my best behavior."

I exhaled a hard breath as I looked up at him from under my lashes. "Well, that's disappointing."

Sugar stretched, and behind me came a sleepy meow followed by, "Breakfast, Mama."

I shook my head at Sin. "I'll throw my robe on and come out."

He nodded knowingly. "Probably better than getting syrup all over the bed. I'll meet you at the diner."

That's what we'd taken to calling the booth in the kitchen.

He walked back out with the coffee and pancakes. "Come on, Sugar. Come on, Spider. Breakfast."

"Chicken Party!" Spider tore past me like his little butt was on fire. Sugar followed.

I pulled on my robe and a pair of fuzzy socks. Not that I needed them. One of the nicest things about the RV was the heated floors. Winter elves might do just fine in the cold, but that didn't mean we didn't like creature comforts. I wound my hair up into a clip, then straightened the covers. Not exactly making the bed, but I hadn't had coffee yet either.

I slid into my side of the booth. My coffee and pancakes were already there. Sin joined me with his own as soon as he finished splitting a can of Chicken Party between Sugar and Spider.

As they dug in, we did too. I loved pancakes, and Sin was especially good at making them. They were kind of doughnut-adjacent, after all.

I stretched my right leg out and stuck my foot under his thigh as I gave him a grin. "Thanks for breakfast."

The corner of his mouth hitched up, and his eyes had a dreamy, faraway gleam. "You're welcome."

I knew what he was thinking about. Last night. It had been good. But then so had everything lately. I was more than happy. I was *blissful*. And all while in an RV. Who'd have thought? "How many hours of driving are left?"

"About six."

"You want me to drive for a while?"

He pursed his mouth like he was suppressing a laugh.

"What?" I added a little more syrup to my pancakes. You could never have enough. And this was really good maple we'd picked up in Canada. "I said I would last night. And I can drive, you know."

"I know you can. But driving a rig this size…do you *want* to drive?"

To be honest, it wasn't exactly a burning desire. "I'd like to know I could."

"How about when we get to my parents', you drive around there a bit and see how it feels? You can make sure you're comfortable with the beast there. They have lots of space without much danger of you hitting something."

I smirked at him over my coffee. "You think I'm going to hit something?" For all my teasing, he was probably right. At least at his parents' wide-open property, there was a lot less chance of that.

His brows lifted. "Not necessarily, but have you ever driven a vehicle this size? I'd just want you to be confident with it, that's all."

"Good plan. I'm down with that." I ate another bite of pancakes. Syrup dripped off them in golden strings of sugary deliciousness. "I just feel a little bad that you're doing all the driving."

He gave my leg a squeeze. "Don't. I don't mind it one bit. I love driving. Especially this coach. It's really nice." He picked up his coffee. "I'm sure you'd be great at it once you get the feel of it."

"At your parents', then."

"Yes, definitely."

Spider hopped up on the seat beside me and immediately settled in to clean himself. Sugar was still eating.

Sin patted my leg for me to move it. Once I did, he got up to refill our coffee. "Tomorrow evening we do the shop visit, right?"

"Yes. Then we're free and clear. I can't wait to see your parents' new finale."

He sat back down. "Same here. They've been so secretive about this new trick. I can't imagine what they have planned."

"Maybe your dad is going to saw your mom in half."

He laughed. "That's pretty old-school, but it could be a version of that."

"Are you nervous about the shop visit?"

He shook his head. "Not nervous but... I don't know exactly. Still seems weird to me that anyone would want to meet me just because I married you."

I chuckled. "The closer you are to the throne, the more fascinating you become. My dad taught me that when I was a little girl, and it's only gotten more true with every year."

He winked at me. "I'm as close to the throne as I ever want to be."

"You know what?" I leaned in slightly. "To be perfectly honest, so am I. Right now I feel like I could do this forever. I mean, sure I miss my family a little, but living in this coach and getting to spend so much time with you has been way better than I thought it would be. It's like a working vacation, if that makes sense."

"It does." He smiled, obviously happy. "Do you think part of that feeling is because you're anonymous again?"

I thought about that a moment. I couldn't go anywhere in the NP without being known. It was literally impossible when you were next in line for the throne. "It is nice not to be recognized or treated differently because of who I am. No one else here or at any of the campsites has a clue I'm royalty. They just think I'm some chick with blue hair."

"Which is thankfully long enough to hide your ears."

I cut more pancakes as I nodded. "I realize we live in interesting times, but that might make some people do a double take." I shrugged. "Or not. Hard to tell. I guess I could wear my bracelet and hide myself from people. Although, let's be honest. Some of these RVers are a little off-center themselves."

"I don't want you to wear that bracelet unless you want to." Then he snorted. "You're talking about Chip, aren't you?"

We'd met him two nights ago. "That handlebar mustache! And come on, who travels with a monkey? Amazing guitar player, though."

Sin shot me an amused look. "Sweetheart, we travel with two talking cats."

"But no one knows they talk."

Almost on cue, Sugar burped. "All done."

We burst out laughing.

I shook my head. "Yeah, you're right. Strange is in the eye of the beholder. I'm sure Chip's talking about us right now. Or at least talking about you, the normal guy with the weird, blue-haired wife."

Sin bobbed his head back and forth. "Mmm, pretty sure he would have said hot but weird blue-haired wife."

I giggled. "Well, your hot but weird wife needs to shower and get moving or we're never going to get to your parents' house."

"About that. There's a place along the way where we could stop and look at some ancient petroglyphs."

I screwed up my face as I chewed the last of my pancakes. "Rock drawings?"

He nodded. "I realize it's no giant ball of tin foil, but what do you think?"

"I think I'd rather go straight to your parents'. Unless you have a burning desire to see these things."

"Nope, I'm good. I just didn't want you to miss out on any of the local wonders."

"Is it weird that I really want to get to your parents'? I'm excited to see them."

His grin went ear to ear. "Not at all. Makes me happy you feel that way."

I got up, taking my plate and cup to the sink to rinse. The RV had a dishwasher, so I planned to pop them in there when I was done. "You have great parents. Seriously, I couldn't have asked for better in-laws."

"I feel the same. You going to shower now?"

"Yep." I glanced outside through the little window over the diner table. The sky was streaked with pink, and the day looked like it was going to be beautiful. "I should be ready to hit the road in half an hour or so."

He came up behind me and kissed my neck. "You need any help?"

I smiled and played dumb. "Rinsing my dishes?"

"No." His kiss went lower to the curve of my shoulder.

"Getting ready?"

"Not that either."

I turned the faucet off and twisted around to face him, pinning myself between him and the sink. "In the shower?"

He planted a hand on either side of the sink behind me and stared down at me with those dark, dazzling eyes of his. "I just thought we should preserve water."

"Is that what you thought?"

"That and two people could probably shower faster than one."

We already knew that wasn't true. "Sure, anything is possible." I cupped his face between my hands and kissed him. "But if you use up all the hot water before I get the conditioner out of my hair, you're cleaning the cat box for the next week."

He laughed. "Deal. Maybe you should get a head start."

I slipped under his arm. "See you in there."

Chapter Nine

Sinclair

My parents came outside as we arrived. They had a long, slightly curvy drive that led to the front door, then went around to the side of the house, where it split. One side disappeared beneath the house, which was where the garage was.

The other side went around to the guest quarters.

Their home might not have been a palace, but by Las Vegas standards, it was a showplace. And well it should be. My parents' show was as popular as any Vegas act had ever been. Probably more popular than some of them and certainly well-loved for its mix of funny, creepy, sexy magic.

There was nothing else like it, and fans were rabid.

Which was partly why their estate was gated and had great security. Of course, I'd just punched in my personal code and opened those gates. But no one else would have been able to get through so easily.

With fifteen acres of land, eight thousand square feet for the main house, and another twenty-eight hundred for the guest house, Oasis Grand, as their estate was known, was almost a resort unto itself. They'd named it after the Oasis Casino, because their show there was what had made the house possible.

Jayne waved from the passenger's seat. "Did you tell them we were bringing the cats?"

"Yep. But I also told them we were just going to stay in the RV, so I don't think they set up anything in the guest house."

Thankfully, Spider and Sugar were passed out in the back somewhere, so we wouldn't have to tell them they couldn't come out. I parked, the soft hiss of the hydraulic brakes reassuring me that the bus was secure.

Jayne was already at the door. She practically hopped down the steps as they extended from the coach. "Hi!"

My parents were smiling, which made me smile. I followed my wife, who was already hugging my mom. "Hey, Dad."

"How was the trip?"

"Really good."

He gazed up at the coach. "That's quite a ride you've got there."

"Yeah, it's something else. You want the tour?"

"I'd love it."

I'd already known he would. He loved cars, but vehicles of any kind interested him. "Come on, I'll show you around."

"Great. Then we need to get going."

I stopped in my tracks. "For where?"

"For the show. Your mom and I have to get ready. You two don't need to come until closer to curtain, of course. Your tickets are waiting at Will Call so no need to rush."

"Jayne and I aren't coming to the show tonight. We're coming tomorrow when you debut the new trick. We have to do our official visit at the toy store this evening."

"Oh." My dad frowned. "I guess we got our wires crossed. The Vanishing Woman is debuting tonight."

Like most magicians, my dad named all his illusions. "Tonight?" I really didn't want to miss it.

"Don't worry about it. You can catch it tomorrow."

"The show is at nine, right?"

"Right."

I glanced at Jayne, who was deep in conversation with my mom. "Jayne, what time is our visit to the store?"

She looked over. "It can be anytime. I just told them this evening."

"Could we go early? The new trick debuts tonight, not tomorrow."

"It does? Snowballs. We don't want to miss that. Sure, we can go early. But that means we should start getting ready."

My mom pressed her hands together in front of her. "Oh no! Are you sure that won't mess up your schedule?"

Jayne shook her head. "Nope, it's all good. One of the perks of being the princess is changing the schedule when you need to, and no one can say a word. At least not to your face."

My mom laughed. "Wonderful. Maybe after the show we can all get together for dinner. I know it's late, but we keep graveyard-shift hours here in Vegas."

Jayne laughed. "I'm always available to eat."

"This is true," I said.

My mother shot me a look. "Sinclair, that's not nice to say about your wife."

Jayne patted my mom's arm. "No, it's okay, Lila. He's right. I love food. I can pretty much eat anytime."

My mom shook her head, smiling. "Nothing wrong with that."

Jayne hooked her thumb toward the bus. "You want to see the RV before we hop back in there and get ready?"

She nodded. "I'd love to."

"Hey," my dad said. "What are you kids going to use for a car? You can't drive that behemoth down to the strip and hope to find parking. Not easily anyway."

I shrugged. "I figured we'd get an Uber."

"An Uber. And waste money?" My dad made a face. "Take one of our cars."

"You mean like the Lambo?" I teased.

"Sure, if you want."

Jayne's head whipped around. "Do you mean Lamborghini?"

My dad nodded. "Yep."

Her eyes widened. "You have one?"

He grinned. "I have two. I have a few other fun rides if that's not to your taste."

"Wow."

His grin got bigger. "Where do you think your husband got his love of fine automobiles from?"

She crossed her arms as her gaze took on a curious gleam. "So what else have you got in your garage?"

I snorted. "Now you've done it."

My dad shook his head. "Sadly, we don't have time for a full tour of the garage, but if there's a different kind of car you'd like to take, just let me know, and I'll see what I can do. But I promise tomorrow, I will show you all of them."

Jayne was still smiling. "I'm good with the Lamborghini."

"Then I'll go bring it up. Blue or black?"

Jayne glanced at me. "Blue?"

"Blue is great," I said.

"Good choice." He put his hand on the small of Lila's back. "Now show your mom the RV while I get the car."

"Come on, Mom. We'll give you the tour."

"And," Jayne said, "you can see your grandcats."

We all went back into the bus. It wasn't quite as impressive with the slides closed but still pretty amazing. My mom made all the appropriate appreciative noises at all the right times.

She cooed a little when we showed her the bedroom, but that had nothing to do with the bus. "Look at those sweet babies. Hi there, kitty cats. Remember me?"

Sugar and Spider were curled up together on the bed. Sugar only opened her eyes, but Spider lifted his head.

Jayne was all smiles. "They've been great travelers."

Spider yawned, then blinked up at my mom. "Spider grandmama?"

My mom's hand went to her heart. "Oh, I knew he could talk, but he never said a peep when we visited. Yes, Spider, I'm your grandmama. Do you remember me?"

I stiffened. I wasn't prepared for either of the cats to talk. Especially because they approached conversations with the same lack of filter that toddlers did.

And my mother was a zombie. I was a little afraid of what they might say or comment on.

"Spider remember." He got up and walked toward her, stretching along the way. "Grandmama brush Spider?"

Jayne laughed. "Maybe later, baby. We don't have time right now."

My mom scratched his head. "I promise to brush you tomorrow, okay?"

He leaned into her hand, sleepy-eyed once again. "Kay. Tomorrow. Treats now?"

Jayne rolled her eyes. "I'll give you and Sugar treats before we leave tonight."

"Speaking of," I said, "I should pull the bus around by the guest house or dad's going to have a hard time getting any cars out of the garage."

"Go ahead," my mom said. "Unless you need us to sit down and buckle up?"

"No, you're fine. Just didn't want to start driving if you weren't expecting it." I went up to the driver's seat and moved the coach back to the guest house.

By the time I returned to the bedroom, my mom was holding Spider like a baby and he was purring his head off. Sugar was still asleep or pretending to be. Jayne was looking through her clothes, trying to decide what she was going to wear this evening.

At least Spider hadn't made any comments about the way my mom looked. Or if he had, I hadn't heard them. Or she hadn't minded.

My mom could be a little self-conscious about her looks. I knew she took great care of herself and spent a fortune on skin care, but there was only so much moisturizer could do for zombie skin. Although she was religious about her routine. It even included an extensive vitamin regime meant to supply her system with everything it needed to keep her in the best shape possible, inside and out.

She'd been nervous about meeting Jayne for the first time because of being a zombie. Thankfully, Jayne had been incredible about it, and I believed she'd genuinely come to love my mom. Easy to do, because my mom was awesome, but of course, I was biased.

"I hate to break up the snuggle party," I said. "But we should get moving."

"I know," my mom said as she gazed down at Spider. He swatted at a strand of her hair. "But look at this sweet baby. He's adorable. Aren't, you cute thing?"

Spider looked at me. "Spider cute."

"And he knows it," Jayne said.

A knock on the bus door put both cats into alert mode.

"Sin?" my dad called out. "Car's out front for you. Keys are in it."

"Hang on. I'm coming," I called back.

"I'm right behind you," my mom said. "I'll be back, Spider. You be a good boy while your parents are out tonight."

"Spider always good, Grandmama."

She grinned, then waved to Jayne. "See you later."

"I can't wait," Jayne said. "It's going to be a great show, I just know it."

"Fingers crossed," my mom said.

With my mom following me, I headed for the RV's door. "Thanks for letting us use one of your cars, Dad. That's very generous." I wasn't sure he'd ever let me borrow one before. Not one of the sports cars anyway.

He smiled. "Anything for my daughter-in-law."

I snorted. "That seems about right." My mom kissed my cheek as she slipped past. "We'll see you later at the show. Maybe not until after, but we'll be there."

"And then for dinner," my mom reminded me.

I nodded. "It's a plan." Then just for good luck, I added, "Break a leg."

Chapter Ten

Jayne

Vegas felt like my kind of town. Just thinking that made me feel a little traitorous. The North Pole was definitely home and always would be, but the glitz and glamour of Vegas was undeniably *fun*.

Something about the place charged me up. Maybe it was that whole "what happens in Vegas stays in Vegas" bit. Royals didn't ever really get that option. No matter where they were. Even in the palace.

Normally for an official store visit, I would have worn something appropriate for that kind of royal duty. A navy pantsuit with a silk blouse or an outfit similar.

But this was Las Vegas, and we were going to see *Dead Sexy* right after the store visit, and I was feeling, well, a little wild. Also, Sin and I were basically having a second honeymoon, and that kind of energy made me want to wear something more flattering than a standard navy pantsuit.

I mean, there *was* a navy pantsuit on my side of the RV's wardrobe, but I was not putting it on. Not just yet. It was too early in our relationship for my husband to forget I could be hot. Not that he had. But there would be other places that suit would get worn.

Vegas was not it.

That was why I was currently in black satin cigarette pants and an iridescent blue sequined spaghetti-strap tank top that nearly matched the color of my hair. I'd paired the outfit with strappy black heels, and the look was on point. Super sexy and very Vegas.

For the actual store visit, I was going to add the matching black satin suit jacket, which definitely made the outfit appropriate for the royal duty part of the evening. At least for Vegas. If this was Boise, the employees would probably look at me like I'd OD'ed on my aunt Martha's eggnog fudge if I showed up in this.

But in this town, I had a feeling no one would bat an eye.

Sin had given the outfit a second look, however, and that made me feel like I'd accomplished what I'd set out to do. He was still looking, but the fact that he was behind the wheel of his dad's really expensive sports car was starting to make me think I should have already put the jacket on.

I pointed at the windshield. "Sin, honey, eyes on the road. If you wreck this car, your dad will kill us."

"No, he won't. He'll kill me. He won't say a word to you."

"Okay, great, but that's not going to make me feel better."

He sighed. "I'm watching the road. But it's hard to do when my wife looks like a supermodel."

I grinned. "You don't look bad yourself. Kind of like the supermodel's sexy European boyfriend."

His brow wrinkled in amusement. "European?"

"Well, you're doing that whole dark suit, white shirt, no tie thing. Always looks European to me."

"I did bring a tie for the store. That one with the House of Frost crest. And I'm wearing my lapel pin and my fancy fake watch."

I frowned. "What fancy fake watch?"

"The one Davide put in the jewelry case. Wasn't I supposed to wear that?"

I snorted. "Yes, you were, but that watch isn't a fake."

"What?" He sat up straighter. "All of *your* royal jewelry is fake."

"It is, but you can't really fake a Patek Philippe with that many diamonds on it and still have people think it's real."

His gaze darted from the road to his wrist, then

back again. "Are you kidding me? How much is this thing worth?"

I thought about that for a moment. "I'd say... about as much as this car?"

He seemed to be gripping the steering wheel a little tighter suddenly, which I liked, but the look on his face told me it wasn't from some urgent need to drive more safely. "You have to be kidding."

"Nope."

"And I thought my parents were crazy." He shook his head. "Wait. Does your father know Davide gave me this watch?"

"Of course. I mean, I'm sure he does in a big-picture kind of way. He would have approved the purchase, but Davide is responsible for my royal jewels and now, by default, yours. At least until you get a jeweler of your own. Unless you're happy to share Davide with me."

"I'm fine with Davide, I do not need my own jeweler, but we're getting a little off track. Back to the watch. It's kind of crazy that it's so expensive and I'm wearing it."

"Well, we're driving a car that's crazy expensive."

He thought a moment. "Okay, I get it now. I'm just borrowing this watch for the trip."

"No, it's yours. You can wear it whenever you like, but usually the fancy stuff only gets brought out for royal functions. Although my great-great-great-aunt Lynette always used to wear a diamond and moonstone tiara that matched the diamond and moonstone collar she had made for her trained reindeer. I mean *always*. Even to breakfast."

"Galaxy, right?"

I looked at him in amazement. "I can't believe you remembered the reindeer's name."

"I told you I paid attention in my royalty classes. And to you, obviously."

I grinned and reached over to give his leg a little squeeze. "I love you so much."

"I love you too. But next time you give me something to wear that could double as a down payment on a small nation, let me know?"

"Will do." He was so funny. And so handsome.

He winked at me. "You look fantastic, by the way."

He'd already said that, but I wasn't going to mention he was repeating himself. "Thanks. I feel fantastic. Hot husband, hot car, fun night ahead… it's like all my ducks are in a row and they've got diamond-encrusted beaks."

"That might make it hard for them to eat their dinner."

I snort-laughed. "You are most definitely the man for me."

He grinned. "I know what you mean though." He glanced over. "Hot wife, hot car, great night ahead. Not to quote *Titanic* or anything, but I feel like the king of the world."

"Wait until you get in the store and all the employees start treating you like you can walk on water." I crossed my legs in what little space I had. Lamborghinis were high on style, low on cabin room. "Just don't get a big head. That's all I ask."

"You don't have to worry about that." He paused a moment. "Hey, they know I'm a necromancer, right? That's pretty common knowledge, isn't it?"

"Yes. Why? Worried about how some of them might react?"

"Well, you know some of the citizens of the realm weren't too keen."

"That was only a small faction."

"I know. Still has me thinking."

"I promise you, none of these employees are going to feel that way."

"You sound awfully sure of that."

I tipped my head to the side to see him better. "Okay, maybe I shouldn't promise none of them will because I can't read minds, but let's just say I'd be very surprised. For one thing, if they really do think that way, they would be stupid to let it show. For another, the people that work in the shops are generally there because they've earned the position with hard work and dedication. Not only do they want to be there, they love their jobs, they love the North Pole, and they love everything about it."

"Meaning they love you."

"Meaning they already love *you*."

He nodded, clearly taking it all in.

"These are the people who would have happily attended our wedding if given the chance. You have nothing to worry about."

He shrugged a little. "I wasn't really worried. Just curious, I guess."

"I understand." We were just entering the main part of the city now, and the sun was going down, painting the sky with streaks of orange. I sat back to enjoy the lights. I couldn't help but smile.

There was so much to look at. All the big casinos and hotels, all the tourists, and all the other outrageous characters that made up the strip. I definitely hadn't seen enough of it the first time we were here.

The GPS on Sin's phone gave him a few commands, and before long, we were pulling into the valet parking area at the Fashion Show Mall, which was where the toy store was located. We hadn't come by here on our first visit to Vegas, as there had just been too much else to do, but my dad had told me the shop was located near the Lego store.

Seemed like a good spot to me, considering they both catered to a similar audience.

Valet parking this car, however, did not seem like a good thing. "Are you sure it's okay to let someone else behind the wheel of this machine?"

Sin nodded. "It's Vegas. These guys get all kinds

of cars coming through. They know better than to do anything dumb."

"Good point." It still seemed a little crazy to turn over the keys, but then I realized the car ahead of us was a Rolls-Royce.

If they could valet that, we could valet the Lambo.

The Lambo. Like I was so used to being in a machine like this, I couldn't be bothered to use its full name.

Once inside the mall, we checked the directory and found where we needed to go. We were definitely there to boost morale, but I knew my dad and uncle were going to want a report on how the store looked on the outside, if everything was stocked, what the level of cleanliness was like, how the shimmer was working, all of that.

Shimmer was our term for the winter magic we used in the stores. Generally, the most capable of the employees on shift would use their gifts to make it snow. Since the snow was magical, it dissolved instantly as it touched the floor, leaving behind no mess, dampness, or accumulation. Customers loved it, and our stores were known for it. We'd started out just doing it on the weekends, but spontaneous shimmers were becoming more popular.

I was sure everything, including the shimmer, would be perfect. After all, the employees knew we were coming. Why wouldn't it be?

We weren't in the store yet when an older woman came out to greet us. Pale blue hair, pointed ears, rhinestone glasses. Absolutely adorable with a nice touch of boss lady throw in. She gave a little bow. "Good evening, your highnesses. It is an absolute pleasure to have you. Welcome to the Las Vegas location. I'm Miranda Winterberry, the manager."

"We're so happy to be here." I extended my hand. Shaking hands was only acceptable if begun by the highest-ranking royal in attendance. That was me.

She gladly took my hand, her smile warming even further. Maybe she hadn't been sure I'd want to shake hands.

Sin shook her hand next. "It's very nice to meet you, Miranda. Have you been the manager long?"

"Thank you, Prince Consort. This is my fourth year. I'd love to show you the store and introduce you to all the rest of the employees whenever you're ready."

"Perfect," I said. "We'd love to meet them. Lead the way."

An hour later, we'd met everyone, seen every inch of the store, taken lots of pictures and were now headed back to the valet stand. The store had been irreproachably perfect, as I'd imagined it would be. The shimmer had been amazing. Fat, fluffy flakes that drifted slowly enough that each flake could be appreciated for its intricate beauty.

Also as predicted, the employees, especially the female ones, had gazed at Sin with the kind of starry-eyed adoration usually reserved for boy bands or Hollywood celebrities.

He held out his ticket for the valet on duty to retrieve the car.

As the young man jogged away, I looked up at Sin. He had a half-smile on his face and a dreamy look in his eyes. Adoration had a way of doing that to you. "What did you think?"

"Hmm?" His brows lifted as he looked at me.

"About your first store visit? What did you think?"

"It was great. Such nice people. And the store was perfect. I hate to say it, but it was probably better organized and stocked than the one in Nocturne Falls."

I smirked at his comment. "You know that's because we paid them a visit. I guarantee you that if we told Juniper and Buttercup we were headed there for an official visit, they'd have that place whipped into shape too."

"Yeah, that's true." He sighed, a happy little sound. "Very friendly staff."

I laughed. "Very flirty staff, you mean."

He made a face. "Flirty?"

"Don't act like you didn't notice."

His grin gave him away. "It wasn't like I was encouraging them."

"I know. But I warned you. Becoming Prince Consort has made you irresistible."

He put his arm around me and tugged me closer. "Are you saying I wasn't already irresistible?"

"You absolutely were. To me. But now that you have a royal title…" I shrugged. "I saw you smiling. I know you were basking in the adulation."

The valet arrived with the car.

Sin kissed my temple, then shook his head and sighed. "Now you have me worried."

"About what?"

"My giant ego fitting into the car."

Chapter Eleven

Sinclair

I loved teasing Jayne. She was always a good sport about it, and the banter between us was like the glaze on an already delicious doughnut.

I checked myself out in the Lamborghini's rear-view mirror, patting my hair gently. "Look at that. My head just fits."

She poked me in the shoulder, laughing softly. "You're so silly."

I wasn't ready to let it go. "What do you think sounds better? The Prince Consort's Crazies or Sin's Sinners?"

She was giving me that look like I'd lost my mind. "For what?"

"The name of my fan club."

This time she laughed out loud, shaking her

head. "Wait until I tell your mother how fame has affected you."

"Speaking of, we'd better get moving." I got us back on the strip and headed for the Oasis, the hotel casino my parents' show had called home for the last five years. Before that, they'd performed at a few other smaller casinos, honing their tricks and timing into the show it was today.

"Are we going to be late?"

"No, we should be fine."

"We still have to go to Will Call and pick up the tickets. Won't it be mobbed with the new finale happening?"

"Maybe." I pulled into valet parking at the Oasis. "But they won't start without us." That wasn't true, but I couldn't keep from teasing her. "I am the Prince Consort, after all."

She rolled her eyes while smiling.

I handed the keys to the valet, got my ticket, then went around to help my gorgeous wife out of the low car. She could manage on her own, but it was the gentlemanly thing to do. Not to mention that if an opportunity arose to let everyone around us know that she was with me, I wasn't going to miss it.

I gave her my hand as she unfolded herself from the passenger's seat. She had her jacket over her arm along with her sparkly little evening clutch. She couldn't have looked more beautiful.

"All set?" I asked.

"Yep. Lead the way. Just not too fast. Heels."

I offered her my arm, which she took. "I could carry you."

"Don't you dare, Sinclair Crowe. Not unless you want a good zap of cold."

I'd never have done it, but like I said, I loved to tease her. "Just trying to help." We weren't far from the theater.

We also weren't the only ones headed that way. Quite a few people were streaming toward it.

Thankfully, it only took a few minutes of waiting in line to get our tickets and then make our way to the entrance, where we waited to be ushered to our seats, which were second row.

The casino kept a firm grip on the first row, using those tickets as gifts for the big rollers who dropped serious cash. I didn't begrudge them. Second row was just as good, and my parents needed the casino happy.

Of course, there was always Frank Chiarillo, the guy who owned the Crystal Palace, a casino about half a mile away. He'd been trying to poach them for years.

The current act that headlined at his casino combined comedy with magic and food. Tony Tortellini and his Impastable Magic. Corniest name ever. I'd never seen it in person, but I'd watched a few clips on YouTube. He did things like toss pizza dough so high it vanished, put meatballs into a

91

chef's hat and turn them into doves, and make an enormous wheel of parmesan disappear.

His big finish was rolling his assistant through a giant pasta machine.

It was all very tongue-in-cheek and supposedly pretty funny, but again, I hadn't seen it in person. I knew from experience that Tony was jealous of my parents' success. Anytime they were at a function together, he made that very clear. I suppose that was to be expected from the number two guy.

An usher came to check our tickets and take us to our seats. "Right this way, folks."

We followed him to the front and started to make our way to our seats.

"Princess! Sinclair!"

I looked at the older, blue-haired woman in the seat next to our empty ones and smiled. "Hi, Birdie." She'd dyed her hair blue a while back and had been keeping it that way ever since. "What a nice surprise. What are you doing here?"

"Birdie!" Jayne put her jacket on her seat and gave Birdie a big hug. "What *are* you doing here? And why didn't you tell me you were coming?"

"Well…" Birdie looked at the man beside her. "You both remember Jack Van Zant?"

I did. He was a raven-shifter and a witch's familiar, although I guess werewolf-familiar was a better description because he only had eyes for Birdie. His salt-and-pepper hair gave him a very distinguished look that was slightly at odds with his stocky build. "Good to see you, Jack."

He nodded back. "You too, Sinclair."

Birdie's grin was bright. "We just wanted to check out the wedding chapels."

Jayne gasped. "Are you getting married? *Did* you get married?"

"No, no. If and when that happens, we'll do it in Nocturne Falls. But the chapel there is doing really well. Because of that, we came out here to do some research on expanding and to see what kinds of things the chapels out here might offer that we don't yet." She was still smiling pretty big, though. "Strictly research. Combined with a little vacation to see the new finale."

Jayne put her fists on her hips. "It had better be. Because if you get married and I'm not invited, you're in big trouble."

The house lights flickered. "We'd better sit. Show's about to start." Even so, I leaned in. "Why don't you come to dinner with us and my parents after the show?"

Jack looked at Birdie. "What do you say, sweetheart? Sounds good to me."

"Me, too." She glanced at me. "We'd love to. Thank you for the invite."

Jayne squeezed my arm as she whispered softly, "Thank you. That was kind of you."

I shrugged. "Birdie's family." I meant it too.

After all she'd done helping us plan our wedding, we were indebted to her for life.

I wondered if my parents had orchestrated her and Jack being in the audience tonight, knowing that we'd be here as well. I'd have to ask them later.

The house lights dimmed, and seductive but slightly eerie music started up along with fog and atmospheric lighting. The show had begun.

Ninety minutes flew by, and as the end of the show approached, I found myself getting nervous for the big new trick.

Jayne must have been feeling the same thing because she suddenly grabbed my hand hard. Her gaze was glued to my dad on stage.

He was alone under the spotlight and slightly off to the left. "Ladies and gentlemen, if there's one thing the dead understand, it's cold storage."

He gestured dramatically toward the center of the stage. A new spotlight flared to life, illuminating an enormous, crystal-clear block of ice.

I sucked in a breath.

My mother was frozen inside, suspended like a rag doll. Only her hands stuck out from the ice on either side. She wiggled her fingers, the best she could do for a wave.

The audience gasped appropriately, and a hum rose up as all around us, people murmured in speculation of what was going to happen next.

I wasn't sure myself. Jayne's grip on my hand increased.

My father walked up to the block of ice, easily four feet taller than he was. He knocked on the side of it, the thunk of his knuckles reverberating through the theater. Then he walked all the way around it, knocking on the other three sides. "Solid as a rock." He grinned. "Good thing she loves me."

My mom made a thumbs-up with her right hand. Then a thumbs-down with her left.

The audience laughed, but the sound had an edge of nervousness to it.

My dad, ever the showman, paused just long enough to increase the tension. "All right, I guess I should get her out of there."

He snapped his fingers, and an enormous black silk floated down from the ceiling to cover the block of ice almost all the way to the floor. Beneath the silk, my mom's hands moved enough to show she was still in there.

At this point, I knew my parents' magic well enough to know my mom was probably no longer in that block of ice. Somehow.

My dad, who'd gone just offstage during that distraction, returned with a menacing chromed sledgehammer over his shoulder.

The noise from the crowd increased again.

He stopped a few feet from the ice. "What? How do you get *your* wife out of a block of ice?"

He twirled the sledgehammer a few times to show just how weighty it was. He held it out to someone in the front row so they could confirm it was real, which they did. Then he squared up to the block and took a couple of slow practice swings like a baseball player preparing to knock one out of the park.

"On three," he announced. "One…"

The audience counted with him.

"Two."

My mom's hands were still moving under the silk. Pretty sure that was just another of my dad's illusions.

"Three."

He struck the block squarely, and the ice beneath the silk exploded into a million tiny pieces. At the same time, the silk got yanked back up into the ceiling so the audience could see that nothing remained but shards of ice.

My mother was gone.

My father turned, his gaze on the very back of the theater, the cool, calm look on his face telling me that my mom was about to appear there any second.

Like everyone else in the audience, I turned to find her.

A spotlight illuminated the closed double doors we'd come through an hour and a half ago. Any second, she'd open them and walk through.

I glanced at my dad. He didn't look quite as cool

and calm. Then he looked offstage. Had something gone wrong?

I turned my attention back to the doors again.

My father's voice rang out. "Fooled you."

Everyone looked at him in time to see my mother step out from the rear of the stage, just beyond the melting ice shrapnel. She gave a little wave, then went back behind the curtain.

A roar of applause went up from the crowd, and a second later, the curtain fell. I stared at the stage, trying to work out what I'd just seen.

Jayne let go of my hand to clap. She glanced over at me. "Why aren't you applauding?"

I shook my head, the sinking feeling in my gut almost making me sick. "Because that wasn't really my mother on stage. That was another one of my father's illusions."

Chapter Twelve

Jayne

"What are you talking about?"

He shook his head again, looking about as worried as I'd ever seen him look. "We have to get backstage now."

"Sin, you're freaking me out."

"Babe, I'm already freaked out. Come on, we need to move. I have to know what went wrong."

Nothing had seemed wrong to me. Maybe a little delayed, but I trusted that Sin knew his parents' act well enough to know if something had gone amiss. I grabbed Birdie's hand. "Come with us. Backstage. Both of you."

She didn't argue, just told Jack to follow her, and he did. Sin went straight up to security, flashed an ID card I'd never seen before, had a few words with the guard, and we were escorted through.

Sin got on his phone immediately. After a moment, he spoke. "Dad, we're on our way to your dressing room."

He looked at me. "No answer, voice mail."

"Are you sure something's wrong?"

"Yes. For one thing, there was a delay, and the look on my dad's face said that was not supposed to happen. For another, when my mother appeared on stage, she was in black dance flats. She wears those for practicing. For dress rehearsals and stage performances, she wears heels."

I hadn't noticed the change in footwear. It wouldn't have meant anything to me even if I had. I wanted him to explain it in plain detail. "So what does that mean that she was in the wrong shoes? Couldn't she have changed?"

"Sure, but why would she? That would have impacted their timing. What I think it means is that when she didn't come through the theater doors at the back of the house, my father covered by conjuring up the last image of her that he remembered. The only one that would make sense. Her waving to him on stage at their last practice. His magic is strong enough that no one would realize they were seeing an illusion and not mom in the flesh."

Birdie had been listening intently. She hustled a little closer. "Why didn't she come through the doors?"

"I have no idea, and that's what's bothering me,"

Sin said. His brow was furrowed, and something that looked very much like dread darkened his eyes.

"Maybe the timing was just off. That could happen, right?"

"It could," Sin said. "With anyone besides my parents. They're perfectionists."

We reached the dressing room. Sin pounded on the door. "Dad, it's me." The door came open. "Dad?"

We peeked in. There was no one inside. Sin walked through the door for a better look around.

A moment later, Anson came rushing in, cell phone in his hand and a terrified expression on his face. "I was just about to call you."

The poor man looked like he was about to break down.

"What happened?" I asked.

"Lila never reappeared."

Sin nodded. "I know. She was supposed to come through the doors, wasn't she?"

"Yes." Anson swallowed. "Everything else went as planned. I don't know why she didn't come through the doors. I don't know where she is."

"Anson?" Birdie stepped forward with great concern evident in her clasped hands and soft eyes.

Sin's dad looked at her but said nothing.

"I know this is a magic trick and magicians never reveal their secrets, but maybe if you told us step-by-step how things were supposed to go, we could figure out where it went wrong."

He nodded, still quiet. "It's not really a trick, because it's real old-school magic. Some of it is my illusions, but mostly it's Lila's ability to withstand things no human ever could. And a lot of well-timed movements." He reached out for the chair at the dressing table behind him and sat.

A knock on the door had him up on his feet again.

Sin put his hand out. "I'll get it." He opened the door just a crack. "I'm sorry. Mr. Crowe isn't seeing any visitors right now."

"Son, do you know who I am? I'm Frank Chiarillo. *The* Frank Chiarillo. Move aside now. I'm here to talk to Anson."

Sin didn't budge. "I'm not your son. I'm Anson Crowe's. And I don't care if you're Harry Houdini come back to life; my father isn't seeing anyone. Neither is he interested in whatever pitch you're about to make for why the Crystal Palace is a better place for his and my mother's show."

On the other side of the door, Frank sputtered. "I didn't mean any disrespect. I just wanted to offer my congratulations on the new trick. Quite the unexpected ending."

"Great. I'll let him know." Sin shut the door without waiting for a response. "That guy is unbelievable."

Anson scowled. "Tony's show must be losing sales. Frank's been after us hard lately." He shifted his gaze to the floor. "None of that matters. Nothing does. Nothing but finding your mother."

"Go through the trick," Birdie said. She took a seat on the couch opposite him. "Take us through each step so we can figure this out."

"Okay." Anson cleared his throat. "While I spin time out talking to the audience, Lila gets into the block of ice. There's actually a small opening in the top that she squeezes through. We do the reveal and there she is on stage, looking like she's frozen solid."

"So the ice is real?" Birdie asked.

"Yes. Takes two days in a specially built freezer to make those blocks. We have three in process at any given time just in case one cracks or doesn't freeze clear."

"All right, what's next?"

"I knock on the ice, prove it's real. Then I get the sledgehammer, let the audience see that it's also real, then I shatter the block. Just before that happens, Lila escapes the ice via an invisible opening at the back of the block and goes through a panel in the floor just behind the ice. The door is set on a spring hinge so the moment she steps on it, she goes through. It's kind of a slide."

"Clever," Birdie said.

Anson continued. "The slide shoots her down into the lowest level of the theater. There's a big foam cushion she lands on to keep her safe. From there, she accesses a small door that leads into a secret passage that goes under the theater and comes up into another small booth that opens into the theater lobby. Once she's through, there's a peephole so that she can make sure there's no one blocking the door and no one out there that might see her exit."

I seized that idea. "Maybe that's what happened? Someone was out there? Maybe she's still in the booth waiting." But even as the words came out of my mouth, I knew that wasn't what had happened.

Anson shook his head. "No. If she's delayed for any reason, she flips a switch inside the booth that illuminates a tiny red light on the left side of the theater. If I see that, I know to stall until the light goes off and the coast is clear. The light never came on."

"You guys have thought of everything," Birdie said.

I nodded. It sure seemed that way. "We need to retrace her steps."

Anson took a breath. "I already went below to check out the lower level. The cushion still had some shards of ice on it, so the trapdoor definitely opened."

The lines of concern on Sin's face deepened. "We need to check the whole thing."

Anson shook his head. "There's no way she's in that secret tunnel. I'd know it if she was. Your mother and I have a very deep connection. We're soul mates. Always have been."

"But Dad, there might be a clue in there as to what happened to her."

"You're right. I wasn't thinking straight," Anson said. "But that passage is narrow. I wouldn't fit through it."

I raised my hand. "Would I? Because I'm totally willing."

He nodded. "Yes. Thank you." He got up. "Follow me."

He led us through the backstage area, then to a far corner and a set of steps. Down those and we came to the basement of the theater. He turned on a light. It looked exactly like a basement, too. Bare bulbs, unfinished concrete, steel beams, and drywall. There were a few things stored there, boxes, mostly, along with some old props and stage decorations, but it looked decades old.

He took us a little deeper in, and we came to the cushion he'd talked about. The trapdoor and short slide were clearly visible. Around the cushion were a few wet spots on the concrete. Ice that had melted, no doubt.

Birdie took a few steps, crouched down, and picked something up. She turned it over in her fingers. "Looks like a black sequin."

"Lila's costume was covered in them. Sequins, bugle beads, and Swarovski crystals. She has three of them in constant rotation because each one needs to be repaired before the next show. Sometimes she has to change before the show is over. They're delicate because of all the embellishment."

"Then she was definitely here."

Anson nodded. "Now we just need to know where she went." He looked at me, then pointed to a squat door across from the landing spot. It looked more like a cabinet than a door, really. "The tunnel under the theater is through there. I'll be in the lobby, waiting on you to come through. But are you sure you want to do this? Considering your title and all?"

I nodded. "The only title that matters to me right now is daughter-in-law."

Chapter Thirteen

Sinclair

I'd be lying if I said I wasn't nervous about Jayne following my mom's footsteps. After all, her path hadn't led her back to my father like it was supposed to. But I was also nervous that Jayne would find something bad.

I had no idea what that something bad might be. Part of me didn't want to know. And part of me was desperate to find out.

Jayne's willingness to help somehow made me love her more. I hadn't thought that possible, considering how much I already loved her, but there it was.

She went through the little door, giving me a wink and a smile before she disappeared into the darkness, the last bit of light sparking off her glittering top.

I knew the wink was to reassure me, and it did. Even so, I left the door open just in case she needed to retreat quickly.

Thankfully, Jayne had her own serious magic, skills my mother didn't have. Sure, my mom was a zombie, but the ability to eat brains wasn't really a defensive weapon. Not in the way that being able to freeze someone in a solid block of ice was, which Jayne could do without blinking an eye.

My dad headed for the steps. "I'm going to wait for her. I'll be in the lobby."

"Okay." He looked miserable, which I understood, as I was feeling the same way myself, but I could tell my father was blaming himself for whatever had happened. But there was no way he'd done something to cause my mom's disappearance.

We didn't even know how or why she'd gone missing yet.

A couple of seconds later, Jayne popped out through the door again. "Anybody have a flashlight? It's pretty dark in here." She looked at me. "I don't know how your mom did this in the dark."

"Zombies have excellent night vision," I said. "And what about the flashlight on your phone?"

She made a little perturbed face. "The battery died. I forgot to charge it before we left for the store, then I used up the last of it taking pictures for my dad and uncle."

"Here, take mine," Birdie said as she dug into

her purse. She found it and held the phone out. "You should have a way to reach us anyway. In case…just in case."

"Thanks." Jayne took the phone and went back into the passage.

I couldn't just stand there and wait. I got my own phone out, turned on the flashlight and started looking around the area near the cushion.

There was nothing on the floor that seemed unusual. Birdie and Jack, who'd been remarkably silent, helped me look.

Then Jack straightened. "Don't take this the wrong way, son, but is there any reason your mother would want to disappear?"

I almost snapped, but I knew he meant well. "No. They were very happily married."

Birdie pursed her lips. "That's a good question. And one the police will ask."

I shook my head. "We can't engage the police. They won't understand my dad's magic. And the fact that my mother is an actual zombie."

She didn't look convinced. "But if there's foul play involved—"

"I understand, but it's my dad's call."

"Sinclair, I know these are your parents, but in nearly half of all domestic cases, the husband is to blame."

I straightened and gave her a hard look. "Do you really think my father is involved in this?"

She frowned. "No. Anson is a good man who clearly adores your mother. Just getting to know them over the course of the wedding was enough to teach me that. But the odds are the odds for a reason."

"Not in this case they aren't."

Jack nodded. "He does seem to love her dearly. And she him. Say, you mentioned not being able to go to the police because of your dad's magic, but this ice block trick didn't really seem to incorporate much of your dad's illusion ability. He said so himself. It was all tricks and trapdoors and secret passageways."

I hesitated, thinking. "You're right. And that's generally not how my parents do things. I need to ask my dad about that."

The trapdoor above us opened, and my dad and Jayne peeked through. "Come on up," she said.

"On our way."

As soon as we met them on the stage, I started in with questions for my father. "How many times have you practiced this trick?"

"Enough to perfect it," my dad answered. "But not as many times as we have some of the others. That's because of the ice. It takes so long to make those blocks, and we were eager to debut it."

"About that. Why use so little of your own magic to do this trick? Real ice? Mom actually going through a passageway to get back into the theater? Most of the rest of your tricks are all your own

109

illusions. Actual magic. Not smoke and mirrors."

My father sighed. "Part of that is out of necessity. The trick was inspired by our visit to the North Pole, as you know. But creating the block of ice as an illusion just wasn't as impressive. It didn't look right, no matter how many times I tried it, no matter how many ways I practiced it. There was also the matter of logistics and keeping things real for the sake of our cover. Suddenly having a block of ice on stage that hadn't been manufactured for us would be hard to explain."

"I get that," I said. They employed a vast number of stagehands. At least one of them would wonder how that block of ice just appeared.

"The rest is my doing. Right before we came to see you in the North Pole, Xavier from the Dove and Wand called to tell me he had a rare book come in. A book supposedly from Martin Beck's library." He looked at Birdie and Jack. "Beck was Harry Houdini's manager."

They both nodded, instantly understanding.

"Of course, I had to have the book, so I bought it the same day he called. It was fascinating. Many early escapes were detailed, including a few I'd never heard about or seen performed before." He took a breath. "It inspired me to do some actual non-magical magic. Old-school stuff. Your mom agreed. And so, thanks to that book and the trip to the North Pole, the ice block was born."

"I see." My father had always admired the history of the art of illusions. "Who built the trapdoor and the tunnel?"

"The stage manager had the trapdoor built, but the tunnel's been there. Not sure what it was used for before us. Probably other magic acts? This theater has housed a lot of different shows. The Oasis has been here since 1963."

Jayne turned toward my dad. "Could you use your magic to get her back?"

He shook his head slowly. "I wish I could. The best way I can explain it is that my conjuring, when it comes to moving people and things, works like *Star Trek's* transporter beam. I need coordinates."

"Oh, right," Jayne said. "I remember when you came to the North Pole. You needed longitude and latitude."

"That's right. With a new place, that's how it works. Now, I could conjure myself into my dressing room or out to the lobby or even back to the house, but those are all places I am intimately familiar with." He looked at me. "Without knowing where your mother is, I'm helpless."

"We'll find her," Jayne said.

He swallowed. "This is my fault. I could have easily conjured your mother out of that ice and into the lobby, but I was so enamored with the idea of following in the footsteps of the greats that I wanted to do without."

Birdie frowned. "We really need to call the police. The first forty-eight hours are the most crucial."

My dad ran a hand through his hair. He looked utterly destroyed. "I know that's what's usually done, but how do I explain to them that she's actually a zombie? That her look isn't makeup?"

"We can worry about that when they find her," Birdie said.

He stared despondently at nothing. "But I'm also going to have to explain how she went missing despite the fact that an entire audience saw her onstage."

Birdie looked around the theater. "Can you say it was just a projection of her?"

"I could, but if they ask to see the projection equipment or the film used, I have nothing to show them."

"Hmm." She sighed. "I guess the same would be true for telling them it was a body double."

Jack frowned. "Telling the truth won't work. But making up a plausible explanation could backfire as well. Maybe you shouldn't call the police after all."

My father pinched the bridge of his nose. "If someone did this… If someone took her…" Emotion choked off his words.

"We'll find her, Dad." But that was just a platitude. I didn't know how that was going to happen. Not without any clues.

Sad that the best we could hope for was a ransom note.

My father cleared his throat. "Lila won't like it, but I'll need to call the show manager and tell him until she returns, we have to go dark." He looked like he might be sick.

"Why wouldn't she like that, Dad? You don't have a choice."

"No, I don't. But if the show goes dark for more than three days, we're in breach of contract."

Jack huffed out a breath. "Even for something like this? They have to understand the circumstances."

"I'm sure they would, but if I tell them Lila's missing, the next question will be what are the police doing about it."

"And you can't call the police," Birdie said. "So you just have to go dark and risk breaking your contract?"

My father nodded. "But what does it matter? There is no show without Lila." A deep, shuddering exhale left his body. "There is no me without Lila."

Chapter Fourteen

Jayne

My heart was breaking for Sin's dad. He seemed absolutely shattered. I could imagine. If Sin suddenly disappeared, I was sure I'd feel the same way.

Lila was a kind, dear, sweet woman. I couldn't have asked for a better mother-in-law, and I hated how useless I felt.

More than that, I was desperately worried for her. None of us had any idea what had happened to her, and searching the tunnel hadn't provided a single clue. At least nothing I'd picked up on, and I'd looked hard.

While Sin comforted his father, Birdie came up to me. "Do you think I could fit in that tunnel?"

I did my best to be diplomatic. "Maybe. But it's not the roomiest of spaces."

One corner of her mouth hitched up in a

repressed smile. "Not me like this. My wolf form."

"Oh!" I nodded. "Definitely. You think you can find something I didn't?"

"Not sure. I mostly want to see if I can sniff out her trail. I know you've already been through it, but since you didn't find anything I thought—"

"No, go, it's the best idea I've heard so far."

Anson looked over. "What is?"

"Sending Birdie through the tunnel in her wolf form to track Lila." I did my best to sound as optimistic as I felt. Birdie's tracking abilities were excellent. And Anson needed something to cling to. We all did. "It's worth a shot, right?"

Sin nodded. "Absolutely."

Birdie looked at Sin's dad. "Anson, do you have something of Lila's that I could get a strong scent read off of?"

"Yes. I know just the thing. I'll be right back." He rushed off, returning shortly with a bedazzled jean jacket. "She wears this to practice almost every day."

Birdie held the jacket to her nose and inhaled, her eyes shining with the wolf inside her. Then she nodded and handed it back to Anson. "Perfect. I can smell her perfume but also the deeper, more personal scent that's uniquely her. I've got what I need."

"What now?" he asked as he took the jacket back.

Birdie looked around. "Are we alone? I'd hate for a human to see me shift."

"Probably," Anson said. "There might be a few stagehands left, but they'd all be in the back."

"All right. You four go wait for me in the lobby. I'll need someone to open the door to the booth so I can get out. No thumbs, you know."

"Understood," Anson said. "I'll open the door as soon as we get there. The light might help a little too."

"Good." She handed me her purse. "Hold on to this?"

"Sure thing." I took the bag and tucked it under my arm. "Hey, what about the door to the secret tunnel?"

"It's still open," Sin answered. "I didn't close it after you went through."

"Good enough," Birdie said. A shimmer of magic and a few seconds later, a wolf took Birdie's place. She trotted over to the trapdoor and stepped on it.

Her weight opened the door and dropped her through. A small whimper was followed by a little woof, then nothing.

I hoped Birdie hadn't hurt herself, but the noises sounded more like surprise and exhaling than pain.

"To the lobby," Anson said.

We hustled off the stage and through the theater. I hoped that my scent in the tunnel wouldn't throw anything off. I wished we'd sent Birdie through first, just to make sure I didn't muddle anything up. I knew a werewolf's tracking ability was keen, but we didn't need anything else to go wrong.

Anson went straight to the booth I'd come out of earlier. The door was artfully concealed to look like one the lobby's decorative panels. He pushed on it, and it popped open. The mouth of the tunnel looked darker than I remembered.

As we stood there waiting, Sin grabbed my hand and gave it a squeeze. I squeezed back. The air was thick with the hope and tension of the moment. Jack's brows were furrowed. No one said a word.

Before long, we heard the scrabbling of talons.

"Birdie." Jack breathed out the word like he was relieved to hear her coming. Had he been concerned something would happen to her in the tunnel?

Wolf Birdie appeared, nostrils working, eyes bright. She paid no attention to us as she slowed, taking just enough steps to move her out of the booth and into the lobby.

We moved out of her way to let her do her thing. She lifted her snout into the air as if searching. She must have found enough of a scent trail because she took off again, this time across the lobby and to another wall panel.

She scratched at it, pawing insistently.

"Is this another secret passage? Where does this lead?" Sin asked.

Anson shook his head. "It's not anything. It used to be an emergency handicap exit, but when the Oasis remodeled, that all got changed and this was boarded up."

Birdie whined, almost dancing from paw to paw with eager energy.

"Are you sure? Birdie seems to think Mom's trail goes through there. We need to open it," Sin said. "Maybe with that sledgehammer you used on the ice."

"No need. Step back. You too, Birdie." As we moved, Anson held his hands out, his concentration visibly increasing. There was a little cracking of wood, then suddenly, the panel popped open very much like the booth door had. "Hmm. That didn't take as much effort as I thought it would."

There was very clearly a hallway on the other side.

Birdie took off through the opening, her talons scratching on the concrete. We followed down the sloped passage. It was easy to see that it had once been an emergency exit. The red EXIT signs with their dual spotlights still remained to illuminate the corridor should the power go out.

Birdie ran down the incline and made the turn. Keeping our eyes on her, we rounded the hundred-and-eighty-degree bend and went down the last ramp. At last, we came to a stop behind her.

Based on the work trucks and shuttle vans, we were standing in one of the Oasis Resort's service garages. Maybe one that was only used for parking disabled vehicles, because there wasn't any activity. The smell of oil and fuel lingered faintly in the air, but the few shuttle vans that were present had a layer of dust on them like they hadn't been used in some time.

Birdie shifted back to her human form and turned to face us. "Lila's trail ends here. Abruptly."

"Meaning?" Anson asked.

"Meaning there's a good chance she got into a vehicle. I can't tell for sure because there are so many other scents down here. Exhaust and gasoline and all that." She shook her head. "Sorry."

Anson stared at Birdie like he hoped she had answers. "Are you saying she just left? Why would she do that? Where would she go?"

"What I'm saying is I don't think she left under her own power." Birdie glanced at the passageway. "For an exit that's been closed off, I also picked up the strong scent of a man's cologne in there." Regret filled her gaze, and she sighed. "I think Lila might have been abducted. Pretty sure, actually. I'm sorry."

Anson stared at her. His hands clenched into tight fists at his sides. His breathing took on a ragged edge. "Who would do such a thing?"

"Does she have any enemies?" Birdie asked.

"No." Anson spat the word out like it was unthinkable. "Everyone loves Lila. She's kind and generous and a friend to everyone. I can't imagine anyone wanting to hurt her."

"Dad," Sin said. "I think whoever did this might have done it to hurt you."

"Or to ruin your career. Or destroy your show." Birdie's expression changed ever so slightly. "Lila might not have any enemies, but do you?"

A dark glint shone in his eyes, and a muscle twitched in his jaw. "A better word would be rival."

Chapter Fifteen

Sinclair

I didn't wait for my father to say the name I knew was coming. Instead I said it for him. "Tony Tortellini." If that second-rate magician had done this, he was going to pay. "He better not have hurt her. That idiot. I will find a way to make him pay."

"You don't know it's him," my dad said. Then he made a face. "But he'd be my first bet too. Not that he's ever come off like the kind of guy who might do this."

Jack snorted. "That's exactly the kind of guy who might do this. The one you least expect."

"That would be him." My dad threw his hands up. "But who else?"

Jayne caught my attention with a look, making me ask, "You want to go *talk* to him?"

I knew my wife well enough to know she didn't mean talk. She meant go snoop around his property and see if there was any sign of my mom or anything odd going on. "He's not going to be keeping her at his house. If he did do it."

Birdie crossed her arms. "Give me everything you have on him, and with enough time on my laptop, I can give you a list of everything he owns. If he took her, you're right that he won't keep her at his home. That wouldn't be smart. Assuming he's a smart guy, he'll keep her somewhere secure and low-key."

Jack grunted at Anson. "This guy is your competition?"

My father nodded. "He's the headliner at the Crystal Palace. Comedy magic is popular, but his *Impastable Magic* comes in second to *Dead Sexy* every year in revenue." He paused like he was thinking. "You know, if there was ever a night for him to disrupt the show, the debut of our new trick would be the one."

"That makes me think," Jack continued. "If this guy is local and well-known, would he really have done this himself? Seems like a big risk to take. He'd be recognized."

"Good point," I said. "Except he could have worn a disguise. At the opening of his act, he actually comes out looking like an old man, so it's not that far of a stretch. *Or* he got someone to do the job for him, which is more likely."

"It's the only way," my father said. "His show

runs at the same time ours does. So he would have been on stage when Lila disappeared."

"Okay, good point," I said. "Of course, he'd have to really trust whoever he hired. This is the kind of thing that could get him blackmailed for the rest of his life."

Jayne rubbed her hands together. "He's still our strongest lead right now. Let's get Birdie working on locations. Meanwhile, Anson, think hard about who else might do something this stupid. And you should probably go home. On the off chance we're wrong and this wasn't Tortellini, there could be a ransom note or call coming your way."

My dad nodded. "I hate not doing anything, but you're right. I should be home. Just in case."

I looked at Jayne, already knowing she had a plan. "And us?"

"We're going to see what we can see at Tortellini's house or condo or wherever he lives. Can't hurt."

Oh, it could hurt. But Jayne always had a way of getting out of the toughest situations, so I wasn't worried. Besides, all my worry was already focused on my mom.

Jack cleared his throat. "You should take me with you."

I looked at him. "You don't want to help Birdie?"

"She doesn't need my help on the computer. And I can turn into a raven. It's amazing what you can see from an aerial view."

My dad, still looking very grim, sighed. "I know where Tortellini lives. An aerial view could help."

In less than an hour, we had Birdie set up at my parents' house with her laptop, which thankfully she'd brought. My dad was making her something to eat. I wasn't sure if she was really hungry or not, but it gave him something to do besides pace the floor and worry, so I was grateful. Of course, knowing Birdie, she probably was hungry. She and Jayne shared very similar appetites.

Jack, Jayne, and I left in my parents' SUV and headed to Tortellini's. He lived in a fancy gated community not far from my parents. I wasn't sure if that was coincidence or another instance of him wanting to emulate my father's success, but at least we didn't have a long drive.

Thanks to Birdie's quick digging, we had a gate code to get in, too. We also had the cover of night on our side. Even so, we'd changed into dark clothing. Not full-on cat burglar, but dark enough that none of us would be super obvious. Jayne's sparkly sequined top and heels weren't snooping-friendly anyway.

I parked at the neighborhood pavilion next to the community playground. Parking on the street at this hour in this neighborhood could very easily get the cops called on us, but there were a few other cars there so I hoped we'd blend in.

Besides, there was already a car parked in front

of Tony's. If we were lucky, it was whoever he'd hired to kidnap my mom coming to report on how things had gone.

"Let's hustle," I said. "If his hired help is there, I don't want to miss anything. In fact, if that's who that car out front belongs to, we need to follow it when it leaves. Could take us straight to my mom."

"Good thinking. Let's all make sure our phones are on silent," Jayne said. "We don't need someone's ringtone giving us away."

Jack shook his head. "I'm not bringing mine. Gonna leave it in the car, if that's all right."

"Sure," I said. "I'm locking it up."

With that, we all got out. I'd looked at the GPS long enough to know where we were going, so I led the group. It was the stucco monstrosity just up ahead and around the block. Tortellini's house wasn't as big as my parents', nor did he have as much land, but he'd done his best to make it as ostentatious as possible.

I pulled my phone out and snapped a photo of the license plate of the car out front, just in case.

Tony's house might have been the biggest in the neighborhood. It was certainly the best lit, which didn't help us out except that it allowed us to see the property a little better. We just had to be careful to stay in the shadows.

There was no fence except on the rear property line, where the house backed up to a golf course.

Thankfully, the course wasn't lit, so that part was darker and provided more cover. There was also a stone path through the side yard, dividing the house from the thick trees and shrubbery that surrounded the property, but taking that path seemed like too big of a risk. We took a quick look around, then slipped into the greenery to maintain our cover.

Jayne immediately started spitting and waving her hands.

I kept my voice down, but I was instantly concerned. "What's wrong?"

"Spiderweb," she whispered with a grimace. "I'm fine." She wiped at her face one more time.

"Listen," Jack said. "This is a perfect place for me to shift. I can do my own recon around the house while you two do yours here. If I find anything, I'll come right back and let you know."

I shook my head. "No, if it's something good, stay and get all the info you can. Chances are, we'll miss something if you leave."

"All right. Just don't split without me."

"Not intentionally. But if something happens…"

Jack smiled. "It's not that big of a deal. I can fly back to your parents'. That house is probably visible from space, so I don't think I'll have any trouble finding it."

I gave him a thumbs-up. "Good."

"All right. Let's see what I can see." The air wavered, and a moment later, a large black bird flew up from where Jack had been standing. The bird perched on a nearby branch, gave us a nod, then took off.

As he left, Jayne grabbed my arm and leaned in. "Do you hear voices?"

I listened. "Someone's talking close by. But it could be the neighbors. Maybe we can get closer and figure it out."

Together we made our way through the trees and brush along the side of the house until we came to the backyard and the pool. The underwater lights were on, giving the pool an aqua glow that illuminated everything around it. Two people stood near the sliding doors, which were wide open, allowing a glimpse into the house.

The man was Tony Tortellini, and he was actually just inside the house. The woman standing a few feet closer to the pool looked like his assistant Carrie Caruthers, but it was hard to tell. I was used to seeing her in full stage makeup and a spangled costume, although the skimpy two-piece rhinestone-embellished bathing suit she had on wasn't that much different than what she wore on stage.

Although her lower back tattoo wasn't visible in her stage outfit.

"I think that's his assistant," I told Jayne. "Not completely sure."

They looked to be in a heated conversation, so we listened.

Carrie seemed to be pleading with him. She shook her head, making her blond curls quiver. "You said we'd talk. You said after the show."

"That was yesterday. And that's not exactly what I said. Listen, I'm really tired." Tony was frowning, hands on his hips.

"Yesterday, today, what does it matter? A date is a date, right?" She wiggled her hips a little, obviously trying to entice him.

It didn't work.

"It matters because—look, you shouldn't be here, Carrie," Tony said. That confirmed my guess. He looked irritated. "The neighbors will talk."

"Tony, I'm your assistant."

Jayne poked me, nodding that I'd been right.

Carrie continued. "They're not going to talk. There's nothing odd about us hanging out." She put her hands on her hips. "Besides, I have a surprise for you."

"There's something very odd about it when my wife is out of town and you're here in a bikini." He raked a hand through his hair. "Carrie, what we had was amazing and you're a sweet kid, but it's over. I'm trying to make things right between Gabrielle and me. That's why, when you asked about coming over earlier, I said we'd talk about it later. I didn't mean here at my house."

Jack, in his raven form, landed on the roof.

Carrie looked on the verge of tears. "Why now?

Why all of a sudden? What's changed?"

"Because…she's pregnant. I can't leave with a kid on the way. That changes things. You have to understand that."

"I don't have to understand anything except that you're a jerk."

"Hey," he snapped. "I'm still your boss. Unless you want to find another magic show to hire you without a reference. Don't forget I took a chance on you."

"Don't be like that, Tony. You know I love you. You used to love me too."

That seemed to placate him a little. "I'm sorry, kid. It can't be like that anymore, and that's all there is to it."

She sniffed, grabbed up a filmy pile of chiffon that I took to be a swimsuit cover-up and stomped off toward us.

We ducked. I hoped we couldn't be seen from the path that went around the house.

But Carrie trudged on by, obviously too upset to be aware of anything beyond her own broken heart. I felt for her. She clearly had been made to think their relationship was going to be more than…this. And while I'd never liked Tony, I liked him even less now.

Knowing he was a cheater made me think he could very well be behind my mom's disappearance.

"We should go," I whispered to Jayne.

129

"Wait," she said, pointing toward the house.

Tony had come out of the house and had his phone up to his ear. He seemed to be looking around to make sure Carrie had left. "What's up, Lou?"

"Lou Scholtz," I said to Jayne. "That's his manager."

Tony took a few more steps, stopping near the tiki bar by the far side of the pool. "No, I hadn't heard. Really? Missing? Come on, you're sure? They could be starting that rumor for publicity. Think about it. A magician claiming his wife has disappeared? I mean, that's awfully on the nose, isn't it?"

"They're talking about my mom."

"I know." Jayne put her hand on my arm.

Tony shook his head. "Look, if it's true, then I feel for the guy. If it's for publicity, he's a jerk." He nodded. "Yeah, okay. Talk to you tomorrow."

Raven Jack took flight, headed for the street.

There was so much I wanted to talk about, but this wasn't the place.

As if sensing that, Jayne tugged on my arm. "Let's go. Come on."

The muscles in my jaw tightened as I fought my frustration. I nodded, unable to say anything. She led us back.

I followed in that kind of mindless way where my body did what my brain couldn't. I was too wound up with everything I'd heard. I felt like a pot about to boil over.

And Tony Tortellini was going to get scalded.

Chapter Sixteen

Jayne

Sin was mad. And with good reason. For one thing, how did Tony's manager know about Lila being missing? For another, if Tony was a cheater, was it that much more of a leap to become a kidnapper?

Jack, already returned in his human form, waited for us near one of the big trees at the front of Tony's property. It was a lovely, if somewhat over-the-top, house. The whole neighborhood was nice. Nothing like where Sin's parents lived, but that was basically a self-contained resort.

We all exchanged some looks, but no one said a word until we were safely back in the SUV.

Then Sin unloaded. "How does Lou know my mom is gone? There wasn't supposed to be anyone left in the theater, but someone must have overheard. Which begs the question, which one of my parents' stagehands is reporting to Tony's team? Or did one of the stagehands just tell someone and they told Lou? However it happened, I don't like it."

"Who's Lou?" Jack asked.

"Tony's manager," I supplied. "Lou Scholtz."

"Do the stagehands have to clock out when they leave?" Jack asked. "Or maybe there's another way to find out when they left. Parking garage stamp?"

Sin shook his head. "I don't know if they clock out or not. I'll have to ask my dad. The parking garage isn't a bad idea, but a lot of them don't park in the garage. And some take public transportation."

"Maybe Birdie can tap into the hotel's security cams," I suggested.

Sin snorted. "I know Birdie's good, but casino security is next-level stuff. However, my dad might be able to call in a few favors and get the video we need."

He was starting to feel better. I could see it. "Hey, what about video in the lobby? They must have that, right?"

Sin shook his head. "I don't know. Something else to ask my dad about."

I looked back at Jack. "Have you heard anything from Birdie? Maybe she's found something out."

Jack pulled his phone from the seatback pocket where he'd stored it earlier and brought the screen to life. After a moment, he shook his head. "Nothing new."

He shut the screen down. "I guess it doesn't matter as much now. Doesn't seem like Tony had anything to do with it. He sounded genuinely surprised to hear the news, and he didn't know we were listening, so he had no reason to pretend. Unless you think he'd lie to his manager."

"No," Sin said. "They've been together since the very beginning. I don't think there's much they don't share."

I thought about that. "What about Carrie, the assistant?"

"What about her?" Sin said. "You don't honestly think she had anything to do with my mom's disappearance, do you?"

"I don't know. She did tell Tony she had a surprise for him."

Jack laughed softly. "I think that surprise was a little more personal in nature."

Sin smirked. "I'm with Jack on this one."

I rolled my eyes. Such men. "I know what you're saying, but I don't think that's what she was talking about at all. A woman like that, clearly in love and out of her depth, could definitely do something crazy. Especially if she thinks she needs to prove herself to Tony. Just saying I think she's worth checking out."

"Well," Sin said. "You'll be happy to know I got her license plate number."

"Excellent. Let's get it to Birdie and find out

where Crazy Carrie lives. Tony wouldn't risk keeping your mom at his house, but Carrie wouldn't have his resources, so she might."

Sin glanced at me. "You really think so?"

"You want to leave that stone unturned?"

"Nope." He took his phone out and handed it to me. "First picture in my gallery."

I found it and texted it to Birdie with a note requesting she find out who it was registered to. I sent a second text saying Tony might not be suspect number one anymore.

Then I tucked Sin's phone back in his pocket.

"One other thing," Jack said. "I did a quick fly through upstairs. Tony's bedroom has a balcony that overlooks the golf course, and his sliders were open, so I figured, why miss an opportunity."

"Nice," I said, eager to hear what he'd found. Must be something if he was bringing it up.

"There was a contract on his bed. I only took the quickest look at it, but it seemed like it was to renew his gig at the Crystal Palace. It wasn't signed yet, either. It still had those yellow sticky tabs on it indicating where the signatures should go."

"That's interesting," I said. "And it could be enough to give him motive if he thinks getting rid of your mom and dad would open up a spot for him."

Sin's eyes narrowed, and his grip on the wheel tightened. "It could. But Jack's right that he seemed genuinely surprised by the news about my mother.

Which means we're overlooking the most obvious person."

That got my attention. "Who? What did we miss?"

"If something happened to my parents so they could no longer perform their show and the Oasis had to fill their spot, who benefits the most?"

"Tony, right?"

"Sure. But if he's not involved, who else benefits? The same man who somehow knew about my mother's disappearance even though we were the only ones left in that theater. And even if we weren't alone, whoever was there reported to him."

I glanced at Jack, and we said the same name at the same time. "Lou Scholtz."

I whipped my phone out and starting texting as fast as my fingers could go. I filled in Birdie on all the details, asking her to check out Lou Scholtz and find out everything she could. Maybe we were grasping at straws, but we had so little else to go on.

By the time we got back to Sin's parents' house, Birdie was waiting for us.

"Whose information do you want first?" She held up two pieces of paper. "Carrie's or Lou's?"

I put my hand out. "We'll take them both."

Anson stood nearby, looking as worried as he had when we'd left. Sin went over to talk to him and, I assumed, fill him in.

Jack gave Birdie a wink. "Good job, honey."

"Just doing what I do," she said.

"Well, I want you to do more of it." There was no reason to take Birdie off the case. If she could discover anything of use about Carrie or Lou, it could lead us to Lila. That was all that mattered.

"I'm happy to help," Birdie said. "Is there anything or anyone specific you want me to focus on?"

"Just dig in," I said. "Anything you find might be useful. I think Lou is more interesting than Carrie at this point, so start with him, but I'm happy to know anything about them you can find."

She nodded. "Between us, I still don't like Tony. After all, any man who cheats on his wife…"

"I know. And I agree. But he really sounded surprised. Jack can tell you."

"He did." Jack looked at her. "What can I do to help, honey?"

"Get me a mocha latte. With whip. And keep them coming." She smiled at me. "All I need is my laptop and a steady supply of caffeine. Possibly some snacks. Pastries maybe. Or a little chocolate."

Caffeine and snacks were easy. I just hoped she could find something useful. I went over to where Sin was talking to his dad. "I have the addresses."

Sin nodded. "Dad, we should get going. If you hear anything, let us know."

"You'll be the first one I call." Anson took a deep breath. "Find her."

"We're going to do our best." Sin smiled, but

the expression was tight and thin and meant for reassurance that he clearly didn't feel.

I leaned in. "And you'll be the first one we call the moment we have news."

"Thank you."

"Oh, wait. Sin, did you ask your dad about the cameras?"

"No, that slipped my mind." He looked at his father. "Dad, can you get the security cam footage from the lobby for the time when Mom would have come out of the booth?"

"I can, but I don't think they'll help. The lobby is dark at that point of the production, otherwise the light would tip off the audience when she opens the doors to come back in. Besides that, those cameras only show the exterior lobby doors. Not the doors into the main theater."

That wasn't going to help, but I couldn't let it go. "Even so, maybe they picked up something?"

"I'll get them," Anson said.

"Thanks, Dad." Sin clapped his father on the shoulder, then put his hand on my lower back as we walked toward the door. He spoke as soon as we were outside. "I'm worried about him. If something happens to my mom, it will kill him."

I obviously didn't know Anson as well as Sin did, but I was feeling the same way. "It seems like whoever did this definitely could have meant to disrupt the show. That really makes Lou look bad."

"I think so too. I say we start with him."

I looked at the addresses Birdie had given me. "He lives in a place called Sierra Vista. Do you know it?"

Sin sighed. "That's not going to make visiting Lou very easy. That's another high-end neighborhood with security."

"We'll just get Birdie to find a gate code again like we did for Tony."

"Won't work. Sierra Vista has a guard shack. You have to give your name, then they call the person you're going to see. If Lou doesn't want to see us, and why would he at this hour, then we don't get in."

I tipped my head and gave him a sweet smile. "Have you ever known a thing like that to keep me out?"

He laughed softly. "No. But this isn't just a guard gate. Sierra Vista has a wall around the entire neighborhood."

I gave him a look. "Get the RV keys and just trust me."

Chapter Seventeen

Sinclair

Life with Jayne was never boring, that much was for sure. I drove the coach to Sierra Vista, not sure what she wanted me to do next, but then, she didn't seem exactly sure either. I pulled into the parking lot of a drugstore about a block away from the turn into Lou's neighborhood. "Where do you want me to go now? We're basically there."

Spider, who was curled up on her lap, yawned. "Spider go somewhere?"

"No, Spider," she told him. "You and Sugar have to stay here."

"Mkay." He went back to sleep.

"Sin, can you drive around the outside? Around the wall, I mean. Not too fast, though." She was looking at GPS on her phone. "I kind of get the idea of where Lou lives in the neighborhood. I just need to get my bearings."

"Sure." I headed out again, starting my low-speed tour of Sierra Vista's border wall.

"Oh! Pull in here."

"Babe, there is no 'pull in.' This is desert."

She looked up. "Hmm. Well, we have good tires. Get closer to that wall."

Her plan suddenly became clear. "I don't think that's a good idea."

"What isn't?"

"For you to climb on top of the RV and then jump down onto the other side of the wall. How are you going to get back?"

Her intensely blank stare told me all I needed to know. "How do you know that's what I'm planning?"

"Because I know you." I shook my head. "You'll get stuck in there."

She wrinkled her nose at me. "I figured we'd *both* go."

"Okay, so we'd both get stuck. That's not any better. Plus the RV would just be sitting here with Sugar and Spider in it."

She gave me a stern look. "Your mom could be in there."

"Lou wouldn't keep her at his house any more than Tony would."

"Then he won't be home, and we can look for

clues. Come on. We can probably just jump the wall."

"You can. I don't have the extra strength and speed that winter elves do."

She frowned. "I forgot about that. Well, I'm not going in there without you."

"No, you're not." I thought for a second. "What if we set up a meeting with him?"

"Are you serious?"

"Sure. I could tell him exactly who I am and then spin a story that I don't think my parents' current management is doing the best job for them and I want to see what he could bring to the table."

"That's genius. He'd definitely go for that. I think. Unless he'd see it as a conflict of interest, what with already representing Tony."

"It's a possibility. But even if that was going to be his response, I don't think he could stop himself from taking the meeting. Just to see what he could learn."

Jayne's phone rang. She looked at the screen. Birdie's picture was on it. Jayne answered. "Hi, Birdie. What did you find out?"

She listened, nodding. "Interesting. Hang on. Let me put you on speaker." She tapped the screen and held the phone out. "Go ahead."

"Okay," Birdie started. "Carrie Caruthers is quite the wily one with a bit of a past. Aka Cora Bright, aka Krissy Lawton, but her real name is Carolyn Hernandez, and she's had some troubles."

"Such as?" I asked.

"She's got a police record that includes charges for bad checks, fraud, and failure to appear on a shoplifting charge. Believe it or not, she did six months in a New Mexico women's correctional facility."

"Wow," I said. "And Tony hired her knowing all that."

"He might not have," Birdie said. "All of that information was under her other name."

"I think he knew something," I added. "When we overheard his conversation with her, he brought up the point that he'd taken a chance on her."

"Or," Jayne said, "he might have just meant she didn't have previous magician's assistant experience."

Birdie spoke again. "Well, I can tell you this much. She legally changed her name to Carrie Caruthers a year before she started working for Tony. Unless he paid someone to dig into her past, her record wouldn't have come up with an ordinary background check."

My brows went up. "This certainly makes her seem like a possible suspect."

Jayne nodded. "We need to look at her more closely. Birdie, any chance you took a peek at her finances?"

"I did. Nothing exciting. She makes more as a magician's assistant than I would have thought. Oh, and she did spend a couple hundred bucks at a home and garden center recently."

I looked at Jayne, eyes wide. She looked back at me with the same expression. I shook my head. "That doesn't sound good."

"Yeah," Jayne said. "I'm picturing shovels, tarps, rope, duct tape. We need to visit her house immediately. Lou can wait."

I nodded in full agreement. "Thanks, Birdie. Keep digging."

"Will do." She hung up.

I grabbed my phone, pulling up my map app. "Babe, give me Carrie's address."

She read it off to me, and I plugged it into the GPS.

Thankfully, it wasn't too far away. She lived in the kind of neighborhood I expected. Not fancy but not exactly middle class either. No guard, no gate. Unfortunately, the RV was a little conspicuous. I parked a few streets away, and we used the cover of night to walk into the neighborhood unnoticed.

At least I hoped we were unnoticed. I looked around for security cameras but didn't see any. Didn't mean I hadn't missed them.

Carrie's house took us about a ten-minute walk. It was a typical Vegas two-story cookie-cutter starter mansion. Actually, mansion was a bit a stretch. It was a nice house, but it wasn't exactly a palatial estate. Still, probably more house than one person needed.

The house was dark, which wasn't what I'd expected either. After all, she'd just come from Tony's and had been very upset. I thought maybe she'd be sitting around moping with some ice cream or something like that. Maybe a glass of wine. Maybe a whole bottle.

But the lights were off, and the house was quiet. I looked at Jayne. "You think she's asleep?"

Her brows arched. "I can certainly slip inside and find out."

Thanks to her uncle being Santa Claus, Jayne had the ability to squeeze through very small spaces. Like under doors. Or through a cracked window. Actually, it didn't even need to be cracked open. Just so long as air could get through, so could she. The Saint Nick or Santa slide, she called it. That ability was how he got down chimneys and into houses that didn't have chimneys.

I wasn't sure if it made him dizzy the same way it did Jayne, but it usually took her a few moments for her head to stop spinning once she'd done.

Despite that downside, it was pretty handy, I had to say. But handy or not, I didn't like the idea of putting my wife in danger. Just because the house was dark didn't mean the house was empty. "I don't like you going in there if someone's home."

Jayne shrugged. "What other choice do we have? Besides, I have magic. Which I won't even need because I can take Carrie. She's a twig with fake boobs."

My wife had such a way with words. "How about we take a walk around the house first? See what we can see? Then *maybe* you go in from the back so I don't have to stand here on the sidewalk looking like I'm waiting for someone in the middle of the night in a neighborhood I don't live in."

"It's too bad we don't have a dog. No one would question you if you had a dog on a leash."

"Yeah, it's also too bad cats don't work that way. Although this is Vegas, and weird stuff usually gets overlooked."

"Should we go get Spider? He would totally walk on a leash if we asked him to. And promised him treats."

He'd probably bark if there were treats involved. "Not now. Come on, let's have a look at the rest of the house."

We walked around the side. There were parallel grooves in the grass and dirt.

Jayne pointed at them, keeping her voice down. "Something heavy has been carted through here recently."

I nodded. "Definitely. What, though? They're too narrow to be car tires."

"Maybe a wheelbarrow? Or one of those dolly things."

"Wheelbarrow." I didn't add what else I was thinking, about how a wheelbarrow would make carting a body easier.

145

We followed the lines all the way to the backyard, where it became clear a major remodeling job was underway. Bags of mulch and stones, a variety of potted plants, larger ornamental stones, and a pile of split timbers that would probably be used for outlining paths all waited to be put to use.

"I guess we know what she spent her money on at the home and garden store."

Jayne nodded. "I'm kind of glad. Better than finding out she's burying a body." She looked at the house. "I still think I need to get in there."

"I don't know. I just don't think Carrie is responsible. I would like to know for sure, though." My phone vibrated. I pulled it out and checked the screen. "Forget that. My dad just got a ransom note."

Chapter Eighteen

Jayne

Sin drove faster than was probably wise, but I didn't say a thing. We both wanted to get back as quickly as possible. A ransom note was a big deal. I was so glad Birdie was there. She would know what to do as far as keeping the note safe and clean for things like fingerprints and any other evidence that might be collected.

If Anson ever decided to get the police involved. Otherwise, I wasn't sure fingerprints mattered. Unless Birdie could pull them. She probably could. There wasn't much Birdie couldn't do when it came to this kind of stuff.

We finally got back to Sin's parents' house and went inside. Anson, Birdie, and Jack were all in the kitchen standing around the table. The note was front and center. It looked like a standard sheet of nice letterhead, except the part that would have had the business name and address printed on it had been ripped off, leaving a jagged line across the top of the paper.

I peered between Jack and Birdie to read it. The words were scribbled in loopy handwriting, the ink smeared and messy like it had been done in haste.

Your wife is fine. She'll be returned soon.

I blinked and reread it. "What kind of a ransom note is that? They don't want money? They don't want anything? Just to take Lila and then return her?"

Sin shook his head. "Makes no sense to me either."

"Birdie, have you ever seen anything like this before?" I asked. "I know Nocturne Falls doesn't have a lot of kidnappings, but what's your take on it? And is there any chance you can get fingerprints off it?"

"My take is that whoever did this has a very different motive than your standard kidnapper. I mean, obviously. They haven't asked for anything. Which means they're getting what they want via different means. As for the fingerprints, no go. I already checked. Whoever sent this wore gloves."

Sin looked as unhappy as his father. "What does taking my mother get them? What does it get anyone?"

I glanced at Anson, his handsome face lined with

worry. There was only one answer I could think of. "It gets...the show stopped."

Anson looked up and nodded. "And if they keep her long enough, it gets us in breach of contract. That's all I can think of."

Jack made a soft, disgruntled noise. "Anyone who considers themselves your rival benefits from that, and you already gave us his name."

"But," Sin started, "we went to Tony's. He genuinely didn't seem like he knew about my mom going missing when Lou brought it up."

Anson's worry turned into anger. "Son, he's a showman. Like I am. If he did this, why would he let Lou know? I realize they've been together a long time, but this is a major crime we're talking about. If he told Lou, Lou would have no choice but to turn him in or become an accessory."

Sin crossed his arms. "Then you think Tony could have done it?"

"I do now."

I touched his arm lightly. "Any chance there are some rubber gloves lying around? I know Birdie looked for fingerprints, but I still feel like we shouldn't touch it in case the police end up getting involved."

"My mom has lots of gloves." He went to the sink, opened the cabinet below and took out a box of latex gloves. "She tries to protect her skin as much as possible considering...you know."

"Right." I grabbed a pair from the box and snapped them on, then picked up the note by the edges of the paper and held it to the light.

"Just so you know," Birdie said, "I didn't let anyone else touch it either, except for Anson, who'd already opened the envelope. Just in case, like you said, it ends up going to the police as evidence."

"Sorry about that," Anson said. "I should have been more careful."

"No big deal," I said. "How did the note arrive?"

"Messenger," Anson answered. "He said Fed Ex to get through the gate, but he wasn't. No truck, no uniform." He leaned in a little. "What are you looking for?"

"Watermarks. Or anything else, really, that might tell us where this paper came from."

"Don't you think the top part being ripped off is a clue?"

"Actually…" I squinted, trying to see better. There was something else on the paper where the tear was. "Anyone have a pair of reading glasses I could use? Just a simple pair of magnifiers?"

Jack nudged me, holding a pair out. "Here you go."

"What did you find?" Sin asked.

"Not sure." Pinching the paper between two fingers, I got the readers on. I looked closer at the torn area. "There's the tiniest bit of black here. There must have been something printed on the top of this paper, which was why it was torn off. So it couldn't be identified."

Anson's eyes narrowed. "Will you hold that up to the light again?"

I did as he asked.

He took a long, hard look. "I'll be right back." He disappeared.

When he came back, he was holding another sheet of paper that looked very similar. Except this one was whole and had a short letter typed on it.

"Have a look at this." He held the new sheet of paper up next to the ransom note. Even with the typing, it was easy enough to see that the watermarks matched. Both sheets were the same brand of stationery. The real difference, however, was his piece of paper hadn't had the top torn off and you could plainly see the letterhead.

The intact piece had come from the Crystal Palace casino.

I put the note back on the table. "Birdie, you've got to research this and find out if anyone else uses the same brand of stationery the Crystal Palace does."

She nodded. "I will, but you know this just makes it look even more like Tony or Lou is involved in this."

"I agree."

"I'll kill them both," Anson muttered. "How dare they put my wife in jeopardy?"

I put my hands up. "Okay, hang on. We're just speculating right now. No one should be killing anybody. I know you're beyond angry, Anson—we all are—but we need Lila home safe *with* you, not visiting you in jail."

"She's right, Dad," Sin said. "In fact, I know a way you can help us. I was going to make up a reason to go see Lou, but you could do it for us. He'd see you in a heartbeat."

Anson took a breath. "You think that would help?"

"Sure," Birdie said. "I don't care how cool a customer this guy thinks he is. He's bound to act strangely if the husband of the woman he kidnapped suddenly pays him a visit. Do you know the guy well enough to tell if he's behaving nervously or in some weird way?"

"I think so. We've interacted socially enough times."

Sin nodded. "Good. Call him up, Dad. Leave him a voice mail now so you can get in to see him as soon as possible. It would even be interesting to see just how soon he makes himself available."

"Right," I said. "If he's occupied with Lila, that might impact his schedule." I smiled at Sin. "Good thinking, honey."

Anson pulled out his phone and looked up Lou's number. He tapped the screen to dial. After a moment, he spoke. "Lou, this is Anson Crowe. If

you have time to meet, I'd like to see you. Maybe…
talk about what you could offer us. Call me and let
me know when you're available."

He hung up and stared at his phone for a second.
"If I think for a moment that he's guilty, it's going to
be hard not to use my magic on him. In a painful
way."

I grimaced. "Any chance you have a truth serum
spell?"

"No." A dark gleam filled Anson's gaze. "But
I'm pretty sure I could get him to talk."

"You know," Sin said abruptly, "maybe I should
go with you?"

Anson nodded. "Maybe you should. What do I
say to him if he asks where your mother is? How
do I answer him if he tells me he's heard she's gone
missing?"

We all sort of looked at each other.

Sin made eye contact with me for a moment
before turning back to his dad. "I think you tell him
the truth and see how he reacts."

"But then I'd be confirming what he knows. And
then the world will know what's happened. You
know how fast news like that would travel in this
town." Anson's anger had turned back into hurt.
"Everyone would know she's been taken. That I
couldn't protect her."

"No one will think that," I said. "What happened
to her was in no way your fault."

Birdie nodded. "Jayne's right. The only person who deserves blame is the one who took Lila. She was doing what she was supposed to be doing when she was supposed to be doing it. So were you. That's it. Nothing more, nothing less."

"About that." Jack rocked back on his heels. "Might be time to revisit who on your team knew about that tunnel. And who knew the timing of the trick. Then see if any of their bank accounts have had large payments made recently. Seems to me the timing of this thing would have required a little inside knowledge."

Sin nodded.

"Seems someone might have told Lou something. Could be that someone got a bonus for telling him about Lila." Jack shrugged. "Maybe not. Just a civilian guess."

"And a brilliant one," I said. "Birdie?"

"I'm on it just as soon as Anson can get me a list of employees."

Sin's dad took a deep breath. "I'll do that now."

"Then," Sin said, "maybe you should try to get some sleep."

Anson shook his head slightly. "Try would be all I did. I can't sleep while your mother's out there, who knows where. Probably scared. Maybe even hurt. Or being hurt." He swallowed.

"They're not hurting her." I didn't know that, but I felt it. "First of all, she's incredibly strong. Secondly, the note said she'd be back soon. It read like her disappearance was a temporary inconvenience. Not something she was going to have to recover from. Plus anyone who knows you knows they'd better not hurt her or they will have hell to pay."

Anson looked at me, new confidence in his gaze. "You've got that right."

His phone vibrated. He took it from his pocket and checked the screen. "That was quick. Lou is calling me back." He looked up at Sin. "Let's see how fast he can fit me in."

Chapter Nineteen

Sinclair

Lou managed to fit my dad in at eleven the next morning. Practically dawn by Vegas standards. Earlier would have been better, but an appointment was an appointment, so my dad agreed.

The rest of the night was spent speculating about who was behind my mom's abduction, running every possible scenario we could think of and re-reading the ransom note.

We also helped Birdie dig through employee records. We even went back into employees who'd been fired or who had moved on in the last year. Anyone who might have an ax to grind. Of course, employees that had left in the last year wouldn't know about the new trick, but they might know about the tunnel under the stage.

As had become our guiding motto in this search

for my mom's abductor, we were leaving no stone unturned.

Right around 3 a.m., Birdie announced, "I've got something." She pointed at her computer screen. "An employee by the name of Buck Murphy deposited forty-five hundred dollars yesterday."

My father shook his head. "I'm not sure that's anything more than Buck having a good night at the tables. Pretty sure he spends at least an hour playing blackjack after every shift."

Birdie glanced at my dad. "You think so? That seems like a lot of money."

"Two years ago he bought himself a brand-new Dodge Charger. Paid cash. All from blackjack. Plus Buck's been around a long time. Since before we took over the theater at the Oasis."

"Which means he has to know about the tunnel," Birdie said. "But he's probably not going to do something to mess up his job. Then again..." She shrugged.

I got up and stretched. "He could be worth talking to. Maybe see if he suspects anyone."

Jayne nodded sleepily. "Short-list him for later."

And that was that until dawn broke, when we took a break to eat. No one was really hungry, except Jayne and Birdie, but we made breakfast anyway. Eggs and toast, nothing much. My dad went out and got doughnuts, too. I think more because he needed something to do than for any great desire for sweets.

We'd gone through more coffee, and in Jayne's case, more Dr Pepper, than I think anyone had consumed since the last World Grand Tour Poker tournament.

And, because of everything going on, I brought Sugar and Spider into the house. With my dad's permission, of course. Jayne and I certainly weren't going to be spending much time in the RV with the search for my mom in full swing, and neither of us liked the thought of them being out there alone.

It was nice having them around. The cats were a welcome diversion from the dark cloud hanging over us, entertaining us with their exploration of the house and sudden bursts of speed through certain rooms.

I had a moment where I thought if my mom never came back, my dad should get a cat. Then I almost wept that such a thought had even entered my brain. It made me sick. My mother was absolutely coming back.

I would not think anything to the contrary.

Around ten, my dad and I got ready to meet with Lou. We were going to his office, which wasn't nearly as swanky as his home. It was in a strip mall near Fremont. He liked to tell people that the office brought him good luck because it was the very spot where Tony had walked in one day, looking for representation.

Lou also liked to say it kept him humble.

Truth was, I don't think he spent much time at the office anymore, but I got the luck part. This was Las Vegas. No one made light of such things.

Before we left, I made Jayne and Birdie promise to get some sleep. Even if it was just a twenty-minute nap. I told Jack to keep after them. We'd all be useless if we didn't rest a little.

I drove my dad's SUV with him in the passenger's seat. The silence weighed on me. "How are you doing?" It was a dumb question, but commenting on the weather seemed like an even worse direction to go in.

My father sighed. "Not great."

I nodded. "Me either. But we're going to get her back. And she's going to be fine."

He shook his head. "I want to believe that."

"You should. Listen, you don't know Jayne like I do. She's unstoppable. Especially when she has Birdie's help."

He just stared straight ahead, looking unconvinced.

I was out of words. Didn't matter. There was nothing I could say that would help. We parked outside of Lou's office. A Jaguar sat two spots over, probably his. On one side of his office was the Hunan Palace Buffet. On the other, Lucky's Dry Cleaning.

It was kind of the perfect spot for him.

"You ready?" I asked my dad.

"Yes." He looked at me, his hand on the car

door handle. "But I'll tell you again, if I think he's involved, I'm not leaving without answers."

"If I think he's involved, I'll help you get those answers."

One corner of my father's mouth lifted, the closest he'd gotten to a smile since my mom had failed to appear.

"Come on. Let's see what Lou has to tell us."

We went straight into his office. He had an outer waiting room but no receptionist. The door to the inner office was closed.

"Lou?" My dad called. "It's Anson."

When there was no reply, I went and knocked on the office door. It opened slightly under the pressure of my hand, allowing me a glimpse inside.

Lou was in his chair, slumped over his desk. I shoved the door wide and ran to the desk. "Dad, call 911."

"Already on it."

I put my hand on Lou's neck. There was still a pulse, thankfully. I hauled him back in the chair so he was sitting up. Not the easiest task. Lou was a large man.

My dad was telling the dispatcher what was going on. When he hung up, he joined me at the desk. "Is he…?"

"No," I said. "He still has a pulse. But he's cold and clammy."

"Pale, too." My dad leaned in. "Lou, can you

hear me? Help is on the way."

No response. Lou's eyes were rolled back in his head. I looked at the desk. There were a few prescription bottles and a carafe of water near the phone.

My dad picked the bottles up and read the labels. "A diuretic, blood-pressure meds and some high-cholesterol pills." He grimaced as he looked at me. "Not good. I think it might be his ticker."

The faint wail of sirens filled the air.

"They're going to want a reason why we're here," I told my dad. "What are we going to say?"

"We'll just tell them what I told Lou, that I was thinking about changing management and wanted to see what he could offer."

"And when Maude hears about that?" Maude Dabrowski was my parents' agent. She was a tough cookie and had done well for them, but hearing secondhand that her number-one client was at the number-two agent's office might cause some stress.

My dad put his hand to his forehead. "I still haven't told Maude about your mom."

"Go call her and fill her in. I'll stay here in case the paramedics arrive before you're back."

"Thanks." He walked outside.

I checked Lou's pulse again. Thready but there. I was slightly disappointed for a very selfish reason. If he was dead, I could use my skills to bring him back and find out what had happened.

Not that I thought there was foul play involved. But then again, my mother had just gone missing, he was our number one suspect, and now, right before we were set to talk to him, he was having a major medical emergency?

Life had taught me that there was rarely any such thing as coincidence. Especially in a case like this.

My dad came back to say he'd squared things with Maude just as the paramedics arrived. We got out of the way and let them do their thing. They asked us a few questions but thankfully, nothing too deep. They were emergency services, not cops.

While we waited, I looked around to see what kind of security the strip mall had. Not much. Maybe because of its age, maybe because the landlord didn't want to spring for the tech. But there were no cameras that I could see.

That was disappointing but about what I'd expected.

Lou left on a stretcher, in the back of an ambulance. They'd hooked him up to an IV and oxygen, but he didn't look any better than he had when we'd arrived.

I hated to be pessimistic, but if Lou was the one who'd abducted my mom, things had just gone from bad to worse.

We headed back to the house.

My dad turned in his seat toward me. "You think

we should go by his house? See…what we can see?"

"Jayne wanted to do the same thing last night, and I wouldn't let her. There's no way to get past the guard at the gate, but her idea was to climb up on top of the RV and jump down over the wall."

"I like that girl."

"Dad, that was a terrible idea."

"Head for his house."

"How are we going to get into the community without him to tell the guard we're there to see him?"

My father's eyes narrowed. "You've been living in the North Pole too long. All that cold has frozen your mind."

I wasn't sure what that was supposed to mean, but I drove to Lou's anyway. As we got closer to Lou's neighborhood, the air in the SUV shimmered with magic.

I kept my eyes on road so I didn't miss the turn. "What are you up to?"

"Just smile at the guard if he says anything to you."

The guard shack was just ahead. I looked over at my dad. "Why? What are you—hey." He looked exactly like Lou. I glanced at myself in the rearview mirror. He'd turned me into a hot, busty blonde. "You have got to be kidding me."

"It's just until we get inside. Now put the window down and let me do the talking."

I did as he asked, slowing as we reached the

guard shack. The guard got off his chair and came to greet us.

My dad leaned closer to my open window. "What do you think of my new car?" He grinned wider. "And my new driver?"

"Afternoon, Mr. Scholtz. Looking good." The guard smiled at my dad, but his gaze immediately went to my imaginary bustline. If only he knew.

"Can you buzz us in?" my dad asked. "I don't have a clicker in this car."

"No problem." The guard reached over and pressed a button. The gate started rolling back. "Have a good day."

"You too." My dad straightened and gave the guard a wave.

I put the window up as I drove forward. "I don't even know what to say about that except make me me again, please."

"Not until we get into the house. Can't have the neighbors thinking we're breaking in."

He was right, of course. That didn't make me like my new look any more.

Chapter Twenty

Sinclair

Getting into the house was a no bigger deal than getting into the neighborhood had been. My dad's magic took care of that, too. A little conjuring, and the lock was turned. Honestly, it was a good thing he hadn't chosen a life of crime, because he'd have been a very successful criminal.

Lou's house was nice. I'd expected gaudy, but it wasn't. Lots of creams and beiges and whites except for the pops of color in the modern art that adorned the walls. It was restrained in a way that made me see him a little differently. Like he was more than he seemed to be.

My dad stared up at one of the largest pieces. "That's a Damien Hirst."

"Looks like multicolor dots on a canvas to me.

Let's just check the house for clues and any sign Mom's been here, then get out."

He turned his head. "Son, if Lou can afford a $30,000 painting, why would he be involved in this abduction scheme?"

"Beats me. Does it matter?"

"Yes. I don't think he did it."

"Based on a painting?"

"Look around. This is not the home of a man hurting for money. The idea that he would abduct your mother in the hopes that we'd break our contract and Tony would get moved into our spot makes no sense."

Was my dad right? "Maybe he's got financial worries we don't know about."

"Maybe, but Birdie didn't say anything about that. And if that was true, he's got all kinds of money hanging on these walls. You see any bare spots?"

I looked around. "No."

"If he'd sold something recently, there'd be a place where a piece was missing."

"Okay but could be he just wants to move Tony up."

My father seemed to consider that. "Could be. But Lou isn't a hustler. Never has been. He's got a handful of other clients but all because they know he reps Tony. And he fell into managing Tony because Tony picked him. All Lou did was be in the right office at the right time. I'm not saying we aren't going to look around the house, but I already know we aren't going to find anything."

Twenty minutes later, and my father was right. There was nothing in Lou's house that even hinted of his involvement in my mom's disappearance. The most interesting thing I'd seen was a signed photo of Gabrielle on his office wall. Tony's wife. The pregnant one he was going to work things out with.

I wondered how that was going. Then I wondered if Lou had been instrumental in making that reconciliation happen. I knew he'd been Gabrielle's manager for a few years before she retired. All because of Tony. After they'd started dating, he'd connected her with Lou.

And Lou, wanting to impress Tony, had made a few phone calls, talked to a few people, and somehow Gabrielle rose to the position of principal dancer. I knew all this from my time in Vegas and from things my parents had said. Vegas was a big small town. And in the show circuit, everyone knew everything.

I stared at the picture. She was a beautiful woman. I felt for her. Whether or not she knew Tony was cheating on her, she didn't deserve a husband who couldn't be faithful. And a baby on the way was no guarantee he wouldn't step out again.

My guess was Gabrielle didn't know. But that was based on the fact that Jayne would have killed me if the situation was the same. Of course, I'd never cheat on Jayne. The very idea disgusted me. Why marry a person if you didn't love them enough to be true?

As I joined my dad downstairs in the living room, my phone buzzed. I took it out and checked the screen, instantly answering the call. "Hi, babe. What's up?"

"Please tell me your dad didn't kill Lou Scholtz."

I frowned. "Why would you think that?"

"Because the news is reporting that he just died."

I took a breath as I processed. "You're sure?"

"Yes. Jack was watching it in the other room and came in and told us. It's all over the local stations."

"When we got to Lou's office, we found him slumped over his desk but still alive. My dad's the one who called 911." I shook my head. "I'm so sorry to hear this. We'll be home soon. Love you."

"Love you too." She hung up.

I tucked my phone away, slightly stunned.

My dad came over. "What happened? What are you sorry about?"

"Lou didn't make it. Jayne said they saw it on the local news." I left out the part where she thought my dad was responsible. I probably would have assumed that too, based on my father's statement at the house earlier.

My dad put a hand to his mouth for a few beats, then exhaled. "I wasn't a fan of the guy, but I wouldn't have wished this on him either."

As the shock left me, my senses returned. "Same, but right now, we need to get out of here. We're in a dead man's house. And the guard at the gate thinks he just saw Lou pull in with a hot blonde. When he finds out Lou is dead, that's going to raise some questions."

A muttered curse slipped from my father's lips. "This is going to take a little more magic than the first time."

I didn't ask what he meant, just trusted that he had it handled as we headed for the car. A few minutes later, I understood. He transformed the SUV into a minivan and me into a soccer mom with himself as her son. We left the neighborhood behind without incident, but I didn't like that Lou had now technically been in two places at once.

I drove straight back to my parents' and parked in front of the main doors.

My dad held his hand out. "Keys."

"You going somewhere?"

"No, I just want to put this in the garage and get a different car out for us to use. Just in case."

I held on to the keys. "In case of what?"

He hesitated. "In case it comes up that Lou was seen with a hot blonde when he was supposedly dead in the hospital. And someone decides to check the camera footage for the license plate number, which I didn't use magic to change."

"Dad."

"I know. I didn't think that through."

I cut him some slack, considering everything going on. "Maybe Birdie can help." I hoped.

"You go find out. I'll put the car under wraps."

I gave him the keys, then hopped out, crossing paths with him as he came around to the driver's side. Magic was a very useful thing. Except when it wasn't.

Jayne

"You did what?" I stared at my husband, hoping for an explanation that made sense.

"I didn't do it. My dad did. It's not like he purposefully left the plate unchanged. He just forgot," Sin said.

Birdie snorted for the second time. "I think it's kind of funny."

"Sure," Sin said. "Until you realize if they run the plate, it comes back to my dad. Which is why I have to ask if there's anything you can do about it?"

She eyed Sin like a mother might look at a child who had misbehaved one too many times. "Such as?"

"Such as go into the database and disappear that license number."

She smirked. "Disappear it?"

"You know what I mean," he said.

I nodded. "Please Birdie, can you help? We can't have the police showing up here asking why Lou was driving my father-in-law's SUV."

She sighed with the kind of frustration that was mostly for show. "I'm sure I can do something. But I'm going to need more fuel. Breakfast wore off a long time ago."

"Anything," Sin said. "Name it."

"Cheesesteak sub, *good* fries and a chocolate milkshake. And a nice slice of pie. Or cake. Or both. I'm not picky."

My stomach rumbled. "That sounds good."

Sin smiled. "I'm not surprised."

Anson came in through another door. "What aren't you surprised about?"

"Jayne's appetite," Sin answered.

"You know, we should all eat." Anson looked surprisingly calm for someone who might have the police at his door if Birdie couldn't work her own kind of magic. "We might not feel like it, but we have to take care of ourselves."

"You want a cheesesteak too, Dad?"

"Sure." He nodded. "I bet Jack could go for one, too."

Jack looked up from the tablet he was using in the other room. He had the news still on. "I could."

I approached Anson. "I have to say you seem awfully calm."

171

"You mean about the car?"

I nodded.

He gave me a short, terse smile. "Let's just say that while they might track that plate to this address, they'll never find the car." He looked at everyone. "If that happens, if the authorities do show up, the story is the car was stolen last night. We didn't call the cops because we only discovered it this morning."

Sin crossed his arms. "You hid it?"

Anson nodded. "And it'll stay that way for as long as necessary. Now, let's go get some food."

Chapter Twenty-one

Jayne

Birdie worked through her meal. What she was working on, I wasn't quite sure, but she had given the rest of us assignments to do when we were done eating. Except for Jack. He'd gone to take a nap. I didn't blame him. I'd have done the same thing if I could, but the stress of my mother-in-law's disappearance was too much.

Spider and Sugar had trotted off to the guest room with him. Naps were sort of their thing, and they weren't about to miss the opportunity to sleep curled up next to a bigger warm body. Also, Jack was a raven shifter, and I knew they could smell the bird on him. I wasn't sure, but I had a feeling that was a quality the cats really enjoyed.

Sin and I were to search local newspapers, via the internet, for any past articles about Tony or Lou that might give us insight into where they'd taken Lila, if they had taken her. Birdie wasn't as ready as Anson to let Lou off the hook. Dead or not.

I had Tony. Sin had Lou. We were working year by year, and so far, it was slow going. Most of the articles we found were fluff pieces. Tony at the opening of a business. Tony and Gabrielle at a charity event. Lou giving a one-line quote on the state of show business in town. Boring stuff.

Anson had gone to his office to make the dreaded call to the Oasis about the show being canceled tonight. He'd also have to call everyone involved. Well, maybe not the ushers, but certainly the stagehands, the lighting guys, the makeup people, the… I didn't really know who else worked on a show like that.

Regardless, I suspected he might be in there a while. It wasn't a call he wanted to make for a variety of reasons, one of which being that it made Lila's disappearance real in a brand-new way. He could no longer hope that we'd find her in time for tonight's show. That things would be back to normal with the rise of the curtain.

My heart ached for him. All I could do was pour myself into my work, as boring as it was.

Then, a new article popped up, and it wasn't quite as boring as it had been. "Wow, Tony's wife is beautiful. I can't believe he was cheating on her. Did you know she was a showgirl?"

Sin looked up from the laptop he was working on. He nodded. "More than just a showgirl, she was the principal dancer in the last review featuring showgirls to ever run in Vegas."

I did a quick Google search. *"A Pussycat in Paris?"*

"That was it. Think *Aristocats* in Paris with half-naked women, and you've got the gist of it."

I snorted. "Sounds wildly entertaining."

"It was, until it wasn't. Showgirl reviews couldn't keep up with the big headlining acts, and they were incredibly expensive. The Oasis held on the longest, but obviously even they ended theirs. Wasn't long after that they did the remodel and expanded the theater my parents are in. That's just where the money was."

"It's kind of sad. Las Vegas and showgirls go together like peanut butter and jelly. To me, anyway. They just seem synonymous with each other."

"To most people. Maybe someday someone will bring them back."

"So what happened to…what was her name?"

"Gabrielle," Sin reminded me. "She became Tony's assistant for a while. A lot of the other showgirls stayed in the game by doing special appearances. Birthday parties, conventions, stuff like that. But Gabrielle never did any of that. I think having her in the show helped Tony a lot. Brought in audiences that might not have come to see him otherwise."

"That worked out for him."

"It did, for sure."

"Was he already successful when they married?"

"No, he was just getting started really. In fact, Gabrielle was a bigger star than he was when she joined his show. She absolutely was a part of his success. Just one more reason I can't believe he'd cheat on her."

That raised new questions for me. "Was he cheating back then? Is that why she didn't stay on as his assistant?"

"I'm not sure about either of those things. Maybe she decided to focus on being a wife? Maybe she got tired of working every night? After all, she'd been at it longer than he had." Sin shrugged. "Whatever the reason, she retired from show business altogether after that. And Tony's had a string of different assistants throughout the years. I swear, it seems like he has a new one every time you turn around."

I thought about everything Sin had just told me. "Maybe they get tired of his advances? If that's what's happening. If it is, makes me even sadder for Gabrielle. Why stay with a guy like that? Unless she doesn't know?"

Sin sighed. "Vegas is very much a small town. Word gets around, so I'd be surprised if she didn't at least suspect. But maybe she's just decided to look the other way. And now with a kid on the way? It's not a good situation, that's for sure."

I studied the wedding picture I'd found online. Even in her wedding dress, Gabrielle looked like a showgirl. Tall and beautiful with the kind of sparkling smile that must have been visible from the back rows. "She looks like she's a good bit younger than Tony."

"She is. By probably twelve years. Maybe more."

"Boy," I said. "He has some nerve running around on her."

"Agreed."

I glanced at Birdie, still deep in whatever rabbit hole she'd gone down, then back at Sin. "You know what I think?"

"What's that?"

"We need to look at Carrie again. The new assistant."

His brow furrowed. "As a possible suspect for my mom's abductor?"

I nodded. "Think about it. If she sees her job as disposable, what better way to build job security by proving your loyalty with a little kidnapping of the competition."

"Except that's also crazy."

"No one said she was sane. In fact, that works in her favor. If Tony knows she's a little bananapants, then he'd probably be worried she'd name him as her accomplice if the kidnapping came to light."

Sin's brows bent further. "I could see that."

I held my finger in the air to punctuate my next sentence. "And just because she bought mulch and

177

plants didn't mean part of that order wasn't duct tape and tarps."

He blinked a few times before he answered. Then he checked the time. "Get your shoes on. If we go now, we can catch her before she leaves for the show."

"Or," I said, "should we wait until she leaves and see what we can find out on our own? I mean, is she really going to confess to something just because we're asking questions?"

"Good point. But I'm not interested in waiting. Let's speed the process up."

"How?"

"Follow me." He led me into his dad's office, knocking on the open door so we didn't startle him by just walking in. "Dad?"

Anson turned in his desk chair. He looked miserable. "What can I do for you?"

"I need Carrie to leave early for the show. Jayne and I want to search her house."

He thought for a moment. "Jimmy?"

Sin nodded. "I think that would work."

I didn't have a clue what they were talking about, but it was interesting to watch.

His dad did a quick search on his phone and found Carrie's number, then dialed. "Carrie, darling, I need you to come in early."

And that hadn't been Anson's voice coming out of his mouth.

Sin grinned. He'd told me his father's talents weren't limited to conjuring. He was also a talented mimic, and right now, my best guess was Anson was doing a bang-on impression of someone named Jimmy. At least I assumed it was bang-on. I had no idea who Jimmy was or what he actually sounded like.

Sin leaned over and quietly said, "That's Jimmy Deville, the Crystal Palace's show manager."

That answered that. I couldn't stop smiling. This was very clever.

Anson went on. "Costuming needs to see you. They think one of your outfits shrunk after being cleaned." He hesitated. "I'm sure it'll be fine." Another pause. "That would be great. Might take us a bit to work this out, but have patience, my dear." He nodded. "You are perfection, as always."

Anson hung up, smiling. "That should do it. She sounded overly concerned about the costume not fitting. I know women are sensitive about their weight, but still."

Sin shrugged. "Whatever, it worked."

I nodded. "Anson, that was amazing. Thank you."

His smile disappeared. "I hope you find her."

"We're going to do our best." Sin squeezed his dad's shoulder, and we went back to the living room.

Birdie was still at her laptop. She'd probably be there when we got back, too. I spoke to Sin. "I need shoes."

"And I need keys to a vehicle. Meet you back here in a minute."

I went to the front door and put my flats on, which was where I'd left them. Then I ran back as I realized Carrie's address was in the now well-hidden SUV. "Birdie, we're going out to check on Carrie. I need her address again."

She looked up like she'd only heard half of what I'd said. "The assistant?"

I nodded. "Yes. Why? Is there something new I should know?"

"I was thinking about checking her financials again. Hang on." The computer screen lit up Birdie's glasses as she typed away.

Sin joined me, keys in his hand. "I think I can remember how to get there."

"Wait, Birdie's looking at Carrie's bank accounts again."

Birdie let out a low whistle. "This is interesting. First Buck, now her. But I don't think this is from gambling."

"What?" I felt like I might explode with the not knowing.

Birdie looked over the rims of her glasses at us. "She's had a little windfall since the last time I looked at her accounts. To the tune of ten thousand dollars."

Chapter Twenty-two

Sinclair

Death and ruin. If we found out that Carrie was holding my mother, and we'd already been there once, I was going to be a brand-new level of angry. To think that I might have been that close to my mom and not done anything to help her…

"Why are your knuckles so white?" Jayne asked. "You look like you're afraid the wheel is suddenly going to come loose."

I did my best to relax, but that was easier said than done. "I can't stand to think that we missed an opportunity help my mom. We've already been to Carrie's. If my mom was there and we did nothing—"

"How were we to know?"

"You wanted to go in. And I didn't let you." I exhaled a hot, hard breath.

"Sin, if your dad hadn't called about the ransom note, I would have. This isn't your fault."

It still felt like it. "Regardless, I will never make that mistake again. You can illegally enter and search any place you want from here on out as far as I'm concerned."

"Well, I appreciate that, but we're still acting on a guess. We don't know for sure your mom is there. Or even that Carrie's involved."

"That ten grand looks awfully suspicious."

"It does. From the amount to the timing, it's all kinds of suspicious." Jayne sat back. "I wish Birdie could have figured out where it came from. Or *who* it came from."

The thought of possibly being so close to my mom and doing nothing was making me crazy. I needed to talk about something else. At least until we got to Carrie's house. "What was Birdie working on so diligently this morning?"

"I'm not sure actually. Maybe the license plate? She was pretty focused."

"Did you ask her?"

"No. I didn't want to interrupt her workflow. Do you want me to call her and find out now?"

"I *am* curious. Maybe a quick text wouldn't hurt."

Jayne got her phone out and a second later, her fingers were flying over the screen. Then she waited, eyes watching for a return text to pop up.

Didn't take long.

"Birdie says she took care of the license plate, then she was finding a way into the Las Vegas coroner's office so she could see the determined cause of death for Lou. It just came in about an hour ago. It was ruled a heart attack. Natural causes." She looked up. "She says it was noted that he had a history of high blood pressure and coronary artery disease."

"That jives with the medication that was on his desk." I frowned. "Did she think it was going to be something else?"

"I'll ask." More texting ensued. On both sides. "She says it was just something she wanted to know. She thinks there should have been an autopsy."

"She does?"

Jayne looked at me. "You know how Birdie is. Also, no stone unturned."

"True, but I don't know how to get an autopsy to happen without my dad bringing the cops in and explaining what's happened. I don't think Clark County does them without a valid reason. Obviously. But I mean, it's not standard procedure."

"That might be, but again, this is Birdie we're talking about. If there's a way for her to get an autopsy done, she'll figure it out."

"Tell her to go for it, then."

"Not sure I need to, but okay." Jayne sent another text.

I pulled into Carrie's neighborhood and followed the directions back to her house. I parked a few houses away since her car was still in the drive. I'd have thought she'd be gone by now, but apparently Jimmy's call hadn't motivated her as much as we'd anticipated. I turned the engine off, and we settled in to wait.

Jayne slouched in her seat. "Do you think she'd really leave if she had your mom?"

"What choice would she have? If she doesn't show up for work without a stellar excuse, she'll be in trouble. Especially now that she thinks she's talked to Jimmy and already said she'd come in early. And don't forget, we're working on the assumption that she's done this to impress Tony with her loyalty. If she was willing to kidnap my mom to keep her job—"

"And Tony," Jayne added.

"Right. Then she's not operating under the oppression of logic. She's nuts and is just doing what seems the best for her. So yes, she'd definitely leave my mom alone. Probably tied up and gagged and—"

"Sin, don't go there. You're going to make yourself miserable."

"I already am."

Her eyes held great sympathy. "I know. I am too. I'm trying not to let it make me irrational though."

"You think it's affecting me that much?"

"No. Not yet."

I sat up. "She's getting in her car."

Jayne straightened, too. We both watched until Carrie pulled away. Then my hand went to the car door handle.

"Wait," Jayne said. "What if she forgot something? Give her five more minutes. After that, she'll probably think it's too far to turn back."

"Okay." I was itching to get inside, but being interrupted could cause us big problems. I twisted my wedding ring in nervous anticipation. The minutes went by like hours.

Finally, the time was up.

"Let's go," Jayne said.

I didn't need to be told twice. I was a little concerned that we were doing this in the middle of the day, when neighbors could very easily be watching, but I was more concerned that my mom was inside being held against her will.

I hoped she knew we were doing everything in our power to find her.

All of a sudden, Jayne started calling out. "Charlie! Here, boy. Come to mama."

"What are you doing?"

"The same thing you are because of that neighbor over there getting her mail." Jayne kept a happy smile plastered on her face. "Looking for our lost dog who was headed into the back of Carrie's yard."

My wife. Amazing. I waved at the neighbor eyeballing us. "Charlie boy, come on," I said. "Come to Daddy."

Jayne went as far as to peek behind shrubs and make kissy noises.

The neighbor went inside, and we strolled into Carrie's backyard like we belonged there. Nothing had changed since our last visit. Everything was torn up and in the process of being redone. I supposed that was a good thing. If it had looked like something had been hastily buried, my concern would have skyrocketed.

"We'd better watch where we walk," I said. "Tracking dirt into the house is going to give us away."

"Good point."

We chose our path carefully as we made our way to the back patio and the sliding doors.

"Can you get in through these?"

She looked at me. "Sliding doors? They are notorious for letting air in. Might as well be an open window. Just give me a sec." She looked around. Then she disappeared into a trail of icy vapor that vanished between the doors like smoke being sucked into a vacuum. Knowing she'd inherited the same magic that her uncle, Santa Claus, had only made it that much cooler.

No pun intended.

She materialized on the other side, leaning against the door to brace herself. I knew that particular bit of magic left her lightheaded for a few moments.

After a second, she turned and gave me a thumbs-up, then she unlocked the slider and let me in.

"You okay?"

"Yep. A little dizzy, but it'll pass. You know how it is."

"I do. Should we split up? I'll take upstairs. You look around down here."

"Sounds good," she said. "No basements in Vegas, huh?"

"There are some, but the bedrock here is so hard they're nearly impossible to dig in most places. Or very expensive to dig." Which was how my parents had a garage under their house. "Still, I guess it's worth checking for."

"Okay. Holler if you find anything."

"You too." I went through the house to the foyer, where a set of steps took me upstairs. The house was much splashier than Lou's had been. Very feminine and very Vegas. There were a couple of showgirl headdresses on display as well as a picture of Marilyn Monroe made entirely of colored sequins.

I searched each room. Three bedrooms, two bathrooms and a room with a treadmill, a set of hand weights and some other workout gear. I spent extra time in Carrie's bedroom, looking for clues as to where the money might have come from or any hint that she was involved in my mother's disappearance.

Nothing. Just a bunch of clothes on the bed like she'd gone through a lot of things before deciding what to wear into work. Jayne did the same thing.

Physically and metaphorically empty-handed, I went back downstairs. No sign of my wife. "Babe?"

"In here," she called.

"Find anything?"

"Nothing to indicate your mom's been here, but look at this." She came out of the bathroom that was off the living room holding a little white stick.

"What's that?"

"The answer to two questions. As in I now know why Carrie was so concerned about her costume fitting, and I know what her surprise was." She turned the stick around so I could see the display window. "Tony's wife isn't the only one who's pregnant."

Chapter Twenty-three

Sinclair

"That might explain the money," I said. "After all, if she told Tony about the baby, that could be his way of paying her to keep quiet."

Jayne nodded as she put the pregnancy test on the counter and took out her phone. "That could be the first of many payments. After all, Carrie could sue him for child support."

She took a picture of the stick, then picked it up and went back to the bathroom, presumably to throw it into the trash again.

"You are going to wash your hands, right?" I called after her. "Didn't Carrie pee on that?"

She stuck her head out, clearly amused. "So you do know how those work." She leaned back in, and I heard the water come on.

While I waited, I looked through the mail and

stacks of paper on the counter. Jayne had probably done that already, but I wanted to look anyway. Carrie didn't keep the neatest house.

Jayne came out. With clean hands, I presumed. She nodded at the mail. "Find anything?"

I shook my head. "No. You probably already looked through this stuff, didn't you?"

"I did, but a second glance never hurt. Guess we should head back since we know what Carrie's deal is now."

That made me think. "Could you get DNA off that pregnancy test?"

"You mean to prove it's Carrie's? I don't see why not. Like you said, she did pee on it. Why? What are you thinking?"

"That we need to find a baggie and take that thing with us." I started opening cabinets. "If Tony's willing to pay her ten grand to keep quiet about it, he might be willing to tell us where my mom is. If he's involved."

"Wow, yes, that's a great idea. And at this point, we're running out of suspects, so if he doesn't know anything…forget I said that."

I knew what she'd been going to say. I couldn't dwell on that. Instead, I focused on finding the plastic bags. Cabinet over the stove. I grabbed one, then turned around. But Jayne had been right. "I was thinking the same thing. If Tony can't tell us anything, we're out of luck."

And in this town, that was never a good thing.

I handed Jayne the baggie.

She frowned at me. "I just washed my hands."

"I realize that, but just use the bag like a glove. Don't touch it again."

She took the bag. "Only because I love you. And your mom."

"Thanks."

She went off to retrieve the test, and I tried not to think about us running out of suspects. If it wasn't Lou and it wasn't Carrie and it wasn't Tony, who could it be?

A new name came to me. Why hadn't we thought of him before? Frank Chiarillo. He had motive. He'd been trying to get my parents to come to the Crystal Palace for years. A breach of contract would give him the opening he'd been waiting for.

And he'd been at the show. He'd even come to my dad's dressing room right after. He could have been checking to see how my father was handling my mother's sudden disappearance.

It was completely plausible that he'd kidnapped my mom, stuffed her in a car, then come back in to check on my dad before taking off with her.

New excitement coursed through me. I texted Birdie immediately. *Frank Chiarillo. Owns the Crystal Palace. Find out everything. Please.*

Her reply came fast and short. *On it.*

Jayne returned with the bagged-up test. "You

look happier than when I left. What happened?"

"I figured out who might have my mom if it's not Tony. Frank Chiarillo."

She squinted at me. "Remind me who he is? He owns something, right?"

"The Crystal Palace. He's the guy who came to see my dad right after the show, supposedly to congratulate him on the new trick."

Her eyes went wide. "But he could have been there to check up on how your dad was taking your mom's disappearance. Maybe to see if he'd called the police. I bet if we hadn't been there, Frank might have even offered your dad help. Of course. If Frank helped your dad find your mom, he'd probably think your dad would feel indebted to him. Or something like that."

"Only if my dad had told him my mom was missing. That's the thing. Frank can't act like he knows my mom is missing because my dad covered with an illusion." I nodded toward the door. "Come on, let's walk and talk. I want to get out of here."

"Okay."

We headed for the sliders.

"How are we going to work this?" she asked.

"I already have Birdie looking into him. But first, I want to go confront Tony with this pregnancy test." I opened the slider and went out.

She closed it behind me, locking it and holding up her finger to indicate she needed a second.

Then she slipped through the space between them like she had the first time, materializing next to me. I held on to her, giving her time to regain her equilibrium.

"Let's go," she said. "Hang on to me so I don't fall over but start walking."

I slipped my arm around her waist and got us going. She leaned into me. "You okay?"

"I will be in a minute," she said. "You realize by talking to Tony, you're going to confirm that Lila is missing. If he really doesn't know, he soon will."

"I don't see any way around it."

"I don't either. Maybe your dad should come with us for that conversation. He knows the man better than we do. He might be able to tell if Tony's lying."

"Good idea. I think we should have Birdie and Jack waiting for Tony outside, too. Just in case he is lying, chances are he'll go to wherever he's hidden my mom. If they follow him, we can find her that way."

She straightened as we hit the sidewalk, obviously recovered. "Then that's our plan. And if Tony's not our guy, Frank is up next."

"I'll call my dad on the way and give him a heads-up so he can be ready."

She looked up at me, smiling softly. "I love you."

I didn't know what had brought that on, but I smiled back. "I love you too."

"Let's bring your mom home. Today."

I nodded, a knot in my throat I couldn't swallow. "Yes."

I got us back to the house quickly, calling my dad as promised. We picked him up outside and headed to Tony's. Jack and Birdie followed us, already in on the plan. It had to be weird for my dad to be headed into the home of his rival, but then again, I was sure all he was focused on was my mom.

Didn't help, though, that we had to drive by the Oasis to get there. He didn't say anything about it, just let us know that he'd told Jack and Birdie where to park and what kind of car Tony drove.

We parked, but they continued on, probably to the employee parking lot. We got out and went into the casino. And straight to the theater where Impastable Magic showed.

The doors weren't locked. They never were when something was going on, whether it be a rehearsal or an actual show. Fire laws. We followed behind my dad as he walked down the aisle.

Tony was on stage. So was Carrie. Tony stopped mid-flourish. "Well, well, well. If it isn't the Amazing Anson. What brings you here?"

"First of all, my deepest condolences about Lou."

"Thank you." There was grief in his eyes but a coldness too. "Now if you don't mind, I have a show to get on."

Then my father turned to the matter at hand. "We need to talk. Alone."

194

"Anything you can say to me, you can say right here."

"No," my father said. "I'm not interested in having this conversation with you and your fifty stagehands. Alone."

With a sigh, Tony looked at Carrie. "Take five." Then he hopped off the stage to meet us on the theater level. "How about the lobby?"

"Dressing room would be better."

Looking curious but also a little put out, he rolled his eyes. "Fine. This way."

We wound through the backstage until we got settled into his dressing room. I enjoyed it being smaller and less luxuriously appointed than my parents'.

He closed the door. "All right. What's this about?"

We'd already decided to let my father start the conversation, so Jayne and I stayed behind him. Jayne was actually behind me. Looking hard at Tony's makeup table.

"Is there anything you want to tell me?" My father was taller by about three inches and slightly broader than Tony.

Tony stared at my dad like he was crazy. "About what? You're the one who wanted to talk. Why should I have something to tell you?"

"You're sure?"

"Yes. Positive. I don't know what kind of game

195

you're playing, Crowe, but I have a show to get ready for. So do you. Which does make me wonder why you're not at your own theater."

I could see my father's pulse beating in the vein in his neck. "My show is dark tonight. Do you know why?"

Tony still looked miffed. "Because you're over here, bothering me? Like I don't have enough to deal with."

"Because someone kidnapped Lila."

Tony's annoyance drained off his face, replaced by what seemed to be genuine surprise. "What? When? Wait, Lou said something about that, but I thought it was just a rumor." His eyes widened. "Are you telling me Lila got kidnapped, then the next day, Lou has a heart attack and dies? What's going on?"

My father looked like he was having doubts about Tony's involvement. So was I, frankly. He seemed to be honest in his responses.

My dad took a breath. "We know about Carrie. That you're paying her off to keep the news about the baby quiet. If you don't tell me the truth, I'll make sure everyone knows. Including Gabrielle."

Panic overtook Tony's face. "Wait. You can't do that. Gabi and I are trying to make things right. Well, I am. She doesn't know about Carrie, and I'd like to keep it that way. It's one of the reasons I've been encouraging her to spend so much time at the ranch. It keeps her away from all of this."

196

He took a moment and managed to get most of the panic off his face. "What do you want me to tell you the truth about? You think I had something to do with Lila? I would never do anything like that. I swear on my unborn children."

A beat went by where no one said a word. Then my father crossed his arms. "Then let's call Frank and see what he knows about my missing wife."

Chapter Twenty-four

Jayne

Anson was impressive. It was easy to see where Sin got a lot of his swagger. And in some ways, Anson reminded me of my dad. Anson was, after all, kind of the king of this crazy kingdom called Las Vegas.

Tony nodded. "Yeah, okay, I can do that." He shook his head. "I'm sorry, Anson. About Lila. That's just… I can't imagine."

"And I'm sorry about Lou. I really am."

"I appreciate that, but Lou and I had been on different tracks recently. In fact, we were about to part ways." Tony put his hand on the back of his neck. "He didn't know it, but obviously that doesn't matter now. In a way, I'm sort of glad we never had to have that conversation. Believe it or not, I was supposed to see him earlier today. I was going to take him to lunch. Thank him for helping me see the light about Gabrielle and getting back with her. Then let him down easy."

I looked at Sin. Was that the contract Jack had seen on the bed? A new management deal? Maybe. But did it mean something? I wasn't sure it did. My hand slid down to my purse and the little item I'd helped myself to from Tony's dressing table. But I wasn't about to put it back.

Tony picked up the phone and punched a single button. "Tony calling for Frank. He's not? All right. Thanks." Tony hung up. "Frank's not in his office, but his admin said she'd ping him for me. He's probably out on the floor. Usually he calls back within a couple of minutes."

"Good," Anson said. "We'll wait."

"Sure," Tony answered. He shook his head. "You really think Frank could be involved in this?"

"He's been after Lila and me for years to come to the Crystal Palace. Doing something to break our contract would give him an opportunity. At least in his mind."

Tony's expression grew dark. "He's been trying to poach you?"

"You really didn't know that?" Anson asked.

"No." Tony shook his head, clearly disgusted. He turned away for a moment before facing them again. "Garbage like that is why I was leaving Lou. I liked the guy, but he wasn't protecting me. Okay, great, he talked Gabrielle into giving me another shot, but career-wise, I was finding a lot of my own deals. You know that spot I had on the Kimmel show?"

Anson nodded.

Tony stuck a finger into his chest. "I got that deal. I made that happen. But Lou let people think otherwise. Pretty sure he signed two new clients on that press alone." He sighed. "I just needed someone hungrier. Someone more willing to fight for me."

"I'm not going to argue that with you," Anson said. "Lou had a reputation as a minimal effort kind of guy."

"He was coasting on my coattails." Tony held his hands up. "I don't like speaking ill of the dead, but that's all truth." He made a curious face at the phone. "Frank should have called by now."

Anson shifted with the kind of anxious energy that said he was ready to go. "Tony, I just want you to know that I would never take Frank's offer. The Crystal Palace is yours. Always will be. Even if we lose the Oasis."

Tony nodded. "Thanks. And I really hope that doesn't happen. I mean that."

Anson nodded. "I appreciate that."

Sin shot me a look, brows up. "We should go."

I gave him a quick nod to let him know I agreed. My contraband felt like a glowing neon sign that was getting harder to hide with each passing moment.

"The kids are right," Anson said. "We've taken up enough of your time."

"If I hear anything," Tony said, "you'll be the first to know."

"Thank you, but I'd appreciate it if you'd keep this quiet. This isn't the kind of publicity we want. I'm sure you can understand the difference." Anson's subtext about Carrie wasn't lost on Tony.

He nodded rapidly. "You got it. Not a word. We have to stick together in situations like this."

"Have a good show," Anson said.

"Thanks."

"Oh, and Tony?"

"Yeah?" His brows rose.

"If I find out you're involved in Lila's disappearance and you lied to me, you're going to regret you were born. You got me?"

Tony swallowed and nodded, holding up his hands. "I swear I'm not."

Anson gave him one long, last stare, and then we left, seeing ourselves out.

We headed back to the car the way we'd come in, through the casino. Despite the bells and buzzers and jackpot sirens, I called Birdie. "I don't think he had anything to do with it, but keep an eye on Tony's car for a few more minutes."

"You got it. Headed to Frank's?"

"I think so. Tony called him, but he wasn't in, and he still hadn't returned Tony's call when we left. Makes me think he's busy doing something and he doesn't want to be disturbed."

Sin nodded, agreeing with my assessment.

"All right," she said. "Call if you find anything. Or if you need us."

"Will do, but I don't think we'll need you until we get back. Then I have something for you to look at."

"You got it."

We both hung up. I looked at Anson. "Frank's house? Or one of his properties?"

Anson stopped at the border of the casino floor. "I need to know what else he owns. We aren't going to get many chances to find her. As soon as he realizes we're on to him, he'll move her. Or worse. But she won't be at his house. He wouldn't keep her here. That's too risky."

Sin pulled up the list of properties Frank owned. "There's a lot to cover on here."

Anson was scanning the casino floor. Maybe hoping to catch a glimpse of Frank? "We can rule out any of the places that are going concerns. Like that coffee bar he owns. Too public. Is there anything that looks like a warehouse or a building that's for sale?"

Sin scanned the list. Knowing Birdie, she'd made annotations for that sort of thing. "Here's something. A nightclub near Fremont." He looked up. "It's not operational, as it's currently for sale."

Anson's brows lifted slightly. "Asking price?"

"Two point two million. But there's also a

house listed for sale. Must have been an investment property because it's only twenty-two hundred square feet. Too small for a guy with Frank's money and status."

"Where's the house?" Anson asked.

"Skye Canyon. Looks like it's about thirty minutes away."

"No," Anson said. "He wouldn't keep her there. It's too far away. He'd want something he could easily access. And if the house is for sale, it could be shown anytime."

I tipped my head to one side as I thought about that. "But isn't the same true for the nightclub?"

"Less likely," Anson said. "At that asking price, buyers would have to be pre-qualified. Frank would know if someone was going to look at it, and it's close enough that he could get there first." He took a breath. "That could absolutely be where he's keeping her. Especially because a lot of nightclubs have soundproofing. Even if she yelled for help, no one would hear her."

Sin put his phone away. "Then that's where we're headed."

It took us almost twenty minutes to get there because of traffic. Jack called to say there was still no movement from Tony, which I relayed to Sin and Anson while I kept him on the phone.

"Tell them to go back to the house," Anson said. "Or go out to eat or play tourist or anything else they might want to do. If Lila's not at the nightclub, we're out of options."

That made my heart hurt, but he was kind of right. We'd exhausted all possibilities at this point. And what I needed Birdie for could wait. "Jack? Anson said to call it. He also said you and Birdie should go back to the house or go do whatever you want to do because we're pretty much out of options."

Jack sighed. "I'm sorry."

"Yeah," I said. "Me, too."

"I'll let Birdie know. We'll stay in touch. I think there's something she wants to do anyway."

"Okay, sounds good. Thanks." I hung up and tucked my phone away, pretty much feeling like I was on the verge of a good cry. We couldn't be at the end of this search. We hadn't found Lila yet. Giving up wasn't an option.

But we were sort of out of places to look if the nightclub didn't pan out. Sure, there were more properties to check, but Sin would have said something if another one of them looked like a good option.

My heart sank.

Sin parked outside the nightclub. The place looked like it hadn't been in operation for some time. We got out and took a better look. I left my purse in the car, sticking my phone in my back pocket. Sin shook his head. "We need to find a side entrance. Or a back one. A place we can get into without having the cops called on us."

"I agree, but..." I pointed up at a security camera. "If there's one out front, there will probably be one out back, too."

Anson let out a little grunt. "Child's play." His gaze narrowed, the air shimmered, and a second later, he gave me a nod. "Taken care of."

"Perfect. Let's find that back entrance."

We did, too, down a little side alley and around a corner where there were a couple of dumpsters. Sin looked back toward where we were parked. "I'm going to move the car around here. Just in case we need a quick exit."

"Okay," I said.

He jogged off, leaving Anson and me.

Anson smiled gently. "I know about your ability to enter places. If you'd rather I didn't watch—"

"No, it's fine. What's a little Santa Claus magic amongst family, right?"

His smile grew, and he nodded. "I'd be lying if I said I wasn't curious."

"Well, prepare to be underwhelmed because all you're going to see is a little ice vapor." As tricks went, his were much more entertaining. The Saint Nick slide was boring on purpose. Anything else might draw attention, and that was the last thing my uncle needed on Christmas Eve.

"Still interesting."

"Once I'm in, I'll unlock the door as soon as I get in and get my bearings. Takes my head a few seconds to stop spinning."

"Sounds good. Be careful. We're assuming she's in there alone, but he could have someone watching her."

"I hadn't thought of that. I'll do my best to stay quiet." The back door was a standard metal security door with a push bar lever. "Um, one more thing before I go in. When you did whatever you did to the cameras, did that also deactivate any security system that might have been in place?"

"No, but good thinking. I can do that too." He took a moment and sent a little shiver of magic at the building. "All right, should be good to go now."

"Thanks." I did the Saint Nick slide and went under. Once inside, I leaned against the door while I waited for everything to stop whirling around. Without the benefit of the security lights or windows, the place was pretty dark inside. Typical nightclub, I imagined. The air was stale and stuffy, like it hadn't been circulated for a while.

While I stood there, I listened. Nothing. I made a decision. "Lila?" Worth a shot, I thought, and if Frank did have someone watching her and he came for me, I'd freeze him in place. But there was no answer. Not even a muffled response.

That could be a very bad thing.

I opened the door to let Anson in and saw Sin

getting out of the car. They both came inside. As soon as the door shut, we were plunged into darkness again.

"I called her name," I said. "No answer. Not from her or one of Frank's henchmen."

"She could be tied up and gagged," Anson said. "Or in a room where she couldn't hear you."

"True." I got my phone out and turned on the flashlight. They followed suit. Amazing what that small amount of light did in such a dark, cavernous place. "Split up?"

Anson nodded. "Sin, go check out the front of the house with Jayne. I'll search through the backstage area and the DJ booth."

I didn't think the behind-the-scenes section of a nightclub was really called backstage, but I knew what he meant.

"And remember," he said. "Don't just look for her. Look for signs she'd been here."

I nodded, but as we parted ways, I nudged Sin. "What kinds of signs did he mean exactly?"

Sin took a breath. "My mom's day-to-day routine involves a serious vitamin regime and a lot of heavy-duty moisturizers, balms, and lotions. Living in the desert is hard on everyone's skin, but when you're a zombie, it's a lot worse. She hasn't had the benefit of that routine in twenty-four hours. There's a good chance she's…you know."

"I'm not sure I do." I could hear the reluctance in

his voice. I'd heard it before, the first time he told me his mom was a zombie and he was worried it would make me not want to marry him. "Just say it."

"She's probably shedding."

"Shedding?"

He nodded. "Flakes of skin. I know, it's gross."

I shrugged. "I've been sunburned a few times. I've peeled. It's not that big of a deal. In fact, it might be a good thing. At least we'd know she'd been here."

He smiled, giving me a quick side-eye. "Thanks."

"For what?"

"For not freaking out about the weird stuff."

"You can talk to the dead and I have blue hair, which I think is cool but some people probably think is pretty out there. I'm just saying I'm not sure anything can really be considered weird stuff anymore." I smiled back. "Come on. Let's find your mom."

Chapter Twenty-five

Sinclair

The nightclub was a massive space, and checking all the nooks and crannies took forever. But with each passing minute, I knew the chances of finding my mom grew slimmer. So slim that it was time to face facts. She wasn't there. And there were no signs that she'd been there. So unless my dad turned up something different, we'd finally hit a real brick wall.

Eventually we made our way back to where we'd started. My disappointment was fast turning into anger. The feeling of helplessness made me want to rage.

A juvenile response, maybe, but it was that or break down in a way I wasn't sure I ever had before. I was not prepared to lose my mom. Not when there had to be something else I could do.

My dad joined us a couple of minutes later, the look on his face mirroring my own emotions. "She's not here," he said tersely.

"We didn't have any luck either," Jayne said. "Sin, what other possibilities are on the list?"

I shook my head. "Nothing as promising as this."

She put one hand on her hip. "But maybe he didn't pick this place because it was too obvious."

She was trying to keep us going. And bless her for it, but the darkness hanging over me had gotten its claws into my soul, and I wasn't sure there was any recovering. I didn't say anything.

Neither did my father.

She glanced at my dad, then back at me like she thought one of us would respond. When neither of us did, she frowned. "Snap out of it. Both of you. I know you expected to find her here. So did I. But just because we didn't doesn't mean we're giving up."

My dad looked away.

"Sin," Jayne repeated. "The list of properties."

I couldn't ignore my wife, so I pulled up the list on my phone, the rage turning into a numbness that just barely let me remain functional. I scanned the list. Birdie's notes were helpful, making it easy to eliminate places. "I don't see anything worth investigating."

"It's time to call your Aunt Zinnia," my father said in a small, quiet voice.

Just the idea made me freeze up. I couldn't

process what he was suggesting. The idea that we'd come to that point. "No."

"Sin," my dad said. "At least we'd know."

"Know what?" Jayne asked.

I shook my head. My father could answer her because I wasn't ready to put that explanation into words.

"Lila's great aunt Zinnia is a necro-psychometrist. Basically, by holding or touching something that belongs to someone, she can tell if they're alive or dead. Well. Dead mostly. Death magic runs in Lila's family. It's probably responsible for her turning into a zombie and for why Sin's necromancy is so strong."

I couldn't look at either one of them. Instead, I stared at the floor. "He wants to give Aunt Zinnia something of Mom's and..." I couldn't finish.

The softest gasp escaped Jayne's mouth as she understood what I was saying. "And have her tell you if your mom is...not with us anymore."

I nodded, my throat a knot of emotion that wouldn't let words pass.

Jayne shook her head. "I hate to be indelicate, but isn't your mom...that is, she's a zombie so...isn't she technically already not with us?"

"She's not that kind of zombie," I explained. "She was turned in her teens, and probably because of the death magic that runs in her family, she survived the bite without losing her life. She just changed. She wasn't reanimated, like a zombie that came from someone already deceased."

"Okay," Jayne said. "That makes sense now. Thanks, Sin."

"Sure," I said.

"We should go." My dad gestured toward the exit. "I'll take you back to the house, then go get her."

Aunt Zinnia lived in a retirement community about fifteen minutes from my parents' house. They'd tried to get her to move in with them, but she'd refused, claiming she didn't need anyone to look after her. She didn't either.

But my dad soon might.

Without saying anything else, we all headed for the car. Jayne waited until we were out of the building, then locked the door and slipped back under like she had at Carrie's.

My father drove. I stared blankly out the window, seeing nothing and trying to hold myself together.

If my mother was dead, she would not go unavenged. My skills had a dark side. A side I'd never used because I'd never wanted to or had a reason to. Until now. And now I had both those things, the will and the reason. Or I would, if my mother didn't make it home.

Back at the house, Jayne and I went inside while my dad left to get Aunt Z.

Jayne and I continued on in the same silent status. Moving like we were underwater. Moving with a kind of purposeless aim that seemed more about not breaking down than doing anything meaningful.

Jayne went straight to the couch, where Spider was sleeping, and picked him up, pressing her face into his fur. He didn't seem to mind. Or maybe he knew she needed the comfort he provided.

Birdie and Jack showed up about ten minutes later. Birdie looked at me, sympathy filling her eyes. "No luck, huh?"

I shook my head. "No." I didn't have it in me to explain about my father going to get Aunt Zinnia and what that meant. They'd figure it out soon enough.

"Sorry, son," Jack said.

I nodded. "Thanks."

Birdie went to her laptop. "Don't give up hope."

"I haven't." But even I could hear the gloom in my voice. "I thought you two might do some sightseeing."

Birdie glanced at Jack before answering me. "We did. Sort of. We took a little trip to the Dove and Wand."

"The magic bookstore?"

Jack nodded. "On a hunch, we had a little talk with the proprietor about the book your father bought." He sighed. "That Xavier fellow needed a little convincing, but we still didn't find out much, other than he got it on eBay from a seller by the name of Superfine. Not a lot of help."

Birdie frowned. "I'd hoped for more. I'm still going to dig and see if I can find out who's behind that screen name, but…"

"Right. Doesn't sound like it's going to amount to much." I sat beside Jayne on the couch. "Did you see Sugar?"

Jayne put her hand on my leg. "She's sleeping on the guest room bed."

I felt like I should do something. I just didn't know what. I closed my eyes and tipped my head back, trying to think of what to do next. Jayne leaned in closer, and I put my arm around her. Then she stretched toward me, kissed my cheek, and whispered, "It's going to be okay."

I nodded, but I didn't really believe that, as much as I wanted to.

Jayne got up and went over to Birdie, taking her purse with her. She dug into it and pulled out a bottle of men's cologne.

I frowned. "Where did you get that?"

Jayne lifted one shoulder. "Tony's dressing table. I want Birdie to smell it and see if it's the same as what she smelled in the old emergency exit at the theater."

Birdie held out her hand. "Let me take a whiff."

Jayne gave it to her, and she twisted off the cap. "Serengeti Nights?" She frowned, then held the bottle to her nose. A second later, she grimaced. "Ew. Yes, that's the same stuff."

"So what does that mean?" I asked, twisting around to see them better. "That Tony's a possibility again?"

Birdie looked at Jayne, then back at me. "Could just mean the kidnapper has the same dreadful taste in cologne. Not sure how popular that stuff is, but I know they sell it at most drugstores. It's not exactly designer stuff."

I sank back down on the couch. Another dead end.

When my dad returned with Aunt Zinnia, I got up to greet her. Her expression said that my father had explained on the ride over what was going on with my mom. "Hi, Aunt Z."

"Oh, Sin." She wrapped me in her arms, the familiar smell of her lilac perfume a reassuring comfort. "I'm so sorry. I hope I can give you some good news."

"Me, too." I did my best to give her a little smile as we broke apart. I pointed to Jayne, who'd come over to welcome Aunt Z as well. "You remember my wife?"

"Jayne, of course. How could I forget a princess? Your wedding was the most beautiful thing I've ever seen." She gave Jayne a hug too.

My father gestured toward the back of the house. "I'll go get something of Lila's."

"All right," Zinnia said.

While he did that, I introduced her to Birdie and

Jack. She'd met them at the wedding too but only briefly, so I wasn't sure she'd remember them. She did. She immediately asked Birdie about her grand-niece and grandnephew, proving she and Birdie had clearly spent more time talking than I'd realized.

I let them chat. It meant I didn't have to make small talk, something I definitely wasn't in the mood for.

Jayne came up to me, cupping my face in her hands. "You look like you're on the verge of something not good."

I leaned into her touch, closing my eyes for a moment. "I've never dealt with a situation like this before. If she's gone, Jayne, it's going to change me. I won't be able to rest until I know what's happened." Until I'd punished the person responsible.

"I know. But I don't think she is. We'll figure out who has her. We will. And we'll get her back safe and sound."

"How can you be so sure?"

She smiled, although it didn't reach her eyes. "Because we have to be. Because nothing less is acceptable."

"I wish it was that easy."

She took her hands away. "We just need to think harder. Maybe look at the ransom note again." She frowned. "Sin, when your aunt is done, let's go back to the theater and examine that walled-off exit again. Maybe we missed something."

My dad returned with my mom's phone. As items went, that was about as personal as you could get. He held it out to Zinnia.

She took it and held it close to her heart, closing her eyes.

We all waited, barely breathing.

At last, Aunt Zinnia opened her eyes and shook her head. "I'm not getting anything. Which means Lila's still alive."

New energy and purpose coursed through me. My wife had been right. I needed to listen to her more. I grabbed Jayne's hand. "Come on. We're going back to the theater."

Chapter Twenty-six

Jayne

Aunt Zinnia's announcement confirmed what I'd already thought. Not that I was in any way psychic, but something told me Lila hadn't been done away with. Maybe it was the casualness of the ransom note. Maybe it was my gut feeling. But I refused to believe that whoever had taken her planned to end her life.

Going back to the theater might not give us any more clues, but at least it was something to do until we figured out our next step. Or the kidnapper sent another note.

Or maybe, just maybe, Lila was returned. After all, the note had said she was fine and would be returned soon. We were just now approaching the twenty-four-hour mark. That was soon, right?

Sin was much more like himself. Until Aunt Zinnia's announcement, he'd looked so dark and depressed, I wasn't sure if he was going to be all right. I knew he had abilities I didn't fully understand. The kinds of skills that were the reason some people feared necromancers. But I'd never seen that side of him before.

I didn't really want to, either. Although in this case, if his mother didn't make it home… I wouldn't blame him for whatever he did.

He parked in his dad's spot at the Oasis, and we went into the closed theater. A sign had been posted out front about the show being on temporary hiatus.

Two more days, and they'd be in breach of contract. I thought that through for the hundredth time, but I could only think of three people that really benefited, and one of them was dead.

Tony and Frank certainly looked suspicious, but we'd turned up nothing to connect them in a concrete way.

Sin had gotten the keys from his father, so he unlocked the door and we slipped into the theater. It was cool and dim in the lobby. Only a few lights were on since there was no show.

Sin went right to the hidden panel and popped it open. The passage was dark. Not even the emergency lights were on.

I looked at him. "Did we turn these lights off when we left?" I knew we'd put the panel back.

"No. One of the stagehands must have. Or the casino people."

"But who else would have known they were even on?"

"Good question. You think someone's been in here?"

"Maybe. Seems that way."

"Agreed."

I felt around on the wall just inside the door. "Where is the light switch?"

"Nothing there?"

"Not that I'm feeling."

He turned his phone flashlight on and stepped in to have a better look. Something crunched under his feet. He redirected the light downward as he crouched for a closer look. He picked something up and stood. "What's this?"

He held a tiny broken piece of something dull and beige between his fingers. The color of wheat, kind of. And lightly ridged.

Realization hit me hard. "Oh! It's pasta."

"Why would there be pasta in this hall?" He shifted the piece to his palm and held the flashlight over it. "But you're right. That's exactly what it is."

He shook his head. "You know, one of Tony's tricks is he throws a handful of those little pasta shells at the audience and turns them into confetti before they fall."

"So you're saying he might have pasta in his pockets?"

"He might."

"But would whoever kidnapped your mom have pasta in their pockets? That seems kind of like a stretch. We know Tony couldn't have done it himself. He has a perfect alibi in that he was on stage performing his own show at the same time."

"Right." Sin stared at the broken piece, then crouched again and looked around with his flashlight beam. There were two more pasta shells. "We would have seen these before. Or stepped on them the first time. They have to be new."

"Whoever planted them had to be the same person who turned the lights off." I sighed. "This combined with the same men's cologne seems like Frank to me again. If his plan to break your parents' contract worked, he'd also need to get rid of Tony to make room for them at the Crystal Palace. Framing him for your mom's disappearance could do that."

Sin nodded. "Except my dad never called the cops, which I'm sure Frank expected him to do. If he is the one behind this, it must be killing him that there's no big investigation underway. He'd need that to make things work in his favor."

I stood, which got Sin to his feet as well. "The note makes sense coming from Frank, too. Of course he wouldn't hurt your mom. He needs her. She's half of the act he's desperate to have at his casino."

Sin turned the piece of pasta over in his fingers. "It all fits. The cologne, the pasta, the letterhead…"

"We have to dig deeper into him. Figure out

where he'd have taken her. Are you sure there was nothing on that list of properties that could work?"

"No, I'm not. At this point, we should probably check them all. We have nothing to lose."

I couldn't agree more. I also couldn't stop myself from adding, "No stone unturned."

He called his dad to fill him in, remind him about the note saying Lila would be home soon and to tell him we were going to check all of Frank's properties anyway. Then we left the Oasis behind and started our search. We went to the house that was for sale first.

That trip took us half an hour outside of Vegas. And got us no further along in the search. It was exactly what we'd thought it would be. An empty house. There was no sign Lila had been there, but the countertop was littered with Realtor cards indicating they'd shown the house.

"There's no way he'd think about keeping my mom here," Sin said. "Not with as much traffic as this place is getting."

"Okay, one down. What's next?"

"He's a part owner in the Rare Breed biker bar twenty minutes from here." Sin looked up from his phone. "If my mom is there…"

"Hey, maybe there's an upstairs apartment. Or he's got an office there. Or even a storage closet with a lock. I know it's a long shot but—"

"Yep," Sin said. "We're checking it out."

He was in a better mood. Which made me happier. To be honest, if walking circles in the desert was the answer, I would have done that. Searching multiple properties was no big deal. I didn't hold out a lot of hope we'd find anything useful, but really, we just needed one small thing to link Lila to Frank.

One. Thing. That was all. And Lila was a smart woman. She had to know we were looking for her. Had to know we'd need a clue.

Rare Breed was everything you might think a biker bar would be. Rows of chrome machines filled the front row of parking. Neon beer signs lit the windows, and a scantily clad woman on a Harley-Davidson adorned the bar's sign. Loud music filtered out every time someone opened the door. And a little even when they didn't.

I glanced at Sin as we parked. I should have brought my bracelet so I could blend in better. "You fit in there a lot better than I do."

He snorted. "I don't think so."

"Honey, I have blue hair and elf ears. You're in a black leather jacket with black jeans and black boots. Granted, from the neck up, you look more like male model than some dude who thinks showering once a week is good enough, but I still think you'd have a better chance in there than I would."

Amusement lit his eyes. "Point taken. Good thing I didn't shave today. I'm just going to show the bartenders a picture of my mom and ask if they've seen her. I'll take a look around, too. You staying in the car then?"

"I wasn't planning on it. I was going to check out the back of the place. Can't hurt, right?"

"I guess not. Be careful."

"I swear if anyone threatens me, they'll be an ice cube before they can blink."

"That's my girl." He leaned in and kissed me. "Meet you back here in ten minutes. If you find something, text me. Otherwise, I'm coming to look for you."

"Same," I said. "If you're gone longer than ten minutes and I don't get a text, I will put that whole bar in the deep freeze."

He smiled. "See you in ten."

We got out, and he headed for the front door while I casually went in the other direction and around the back of the property.

More bikes were parked along the side and in the rear parking lot. So were a few cars. Nothing fancy like what Frank might own. I couldn't imagine how he'd come to be a partner in this place. Seemed like a weird financial direction, but what did I know about property in Vegas? Maybe the slots inside got a lot of play. Or maybe he'd won it from someone.

Or maybe…honestly, I had no idea, and I didn't really care. Not since I'd spotted the storage shed at the rear of the property.

I stayed close to the wall and took a good look

around. The bass beat of whatever was playing inside thumped through the walls. I was alone. And thankfully, it was dark. I was about to dart across the parking lot when a young guy with tattoos and a ponytail came out the back, hauling a trash bin filled with bottles.

He dumped them in the recycling, then took his sweet time lighting up a cigarette. I didn't have time to wait around on his smoke break. I focused the tiniest bit of cold on the cigarette's ember, putting it out.

He frowned and relit the smoke. I put it out again. Thankfully, he got frustrated, flicked the cigarette away and went back inside, muttering to himself about cheap smokes.

As soon as the door shut, I jogged over to the storage shed. It was corrugated metal and rusted in most places. There was an old pickup truck parked in front of it. The truck's wheels were flat, and weeds sprouted from under the wipers.

A cursory inspection found the shed had only one door. It was locked. I wasn't really looking forward to going inside because I had no idea what to expect. I tried to peek through the door's one small, very dirty window made of safety glass, but between the wire running through the glass and the dirt caked on it, I couldn't see a thing.

Time was ticking. I had no choice but to slip under the door.

When I materialized on the other side, the smell of gas and oil were almost overwhelming. I fought the dizziness in my head to quickly light up my phone and look around. Metal shelves lined the walls, and they were filled with car parts. Or bike parts. I didn't know enough to tell the difference.

But no sign of Lila. No room to keep her here, either. An old motorcycle frame took up most of the floor space, except for where a chest freezer hugged one wall. Boxes of random restaurant supplies were stacked on top of it.

I couldn't imagine eating anything that came from the Rare Breed's kitchen.

Then I wondered if I should check the freezer. I didn't really want to. But if I didn't, I'd always wonder.

I picked my way over to it, took a deep breath, and hoisted the top up. The smell made me gag. I shone my light inside. Nothing but small, foil-wrapped packages of food that hadn't been fresh in a very long time.

I dropped the lid and went back under the door as quickly as I could. I leaned against the old pickup until my head settled, happily breathing outside air. I checked the time. I had about two minutes before Sin came looking.

I hoped he'd done better than I had. I was disappointed that I hadn't found anything useful. I went back to the car to wait.

He came out of the bar about two seconds after I flipped the passenger-side mirror down to watch for him. He looked both ways, then hustled to join me.

He got in. "Bartenders didn't know anything. I looked around the back of the joint as best I could. Besides the bathrooms, there was the kitchen and a small office, but the door was open, and I could see all of it. She's not there."

"Nothing in the back either, except a shed chock-full of parts and restaurant supplies. And a freezer loaded with gross expired food."

With a curious expression on his face, he pushed the ignition button. "Two down, more than half a list left to go."

Chapter Twenty-seven

Sinclair

The horizon was turning pink as we finished checking out the last property on the list. We hadn't found a single thing linking Frank to my mother, which was frustrating, but Aunt Z's news that my mom was still alive and Jayne's reminder about the note had lifted my spirits considerably.

Which didn't mean vengeance wasn't still on my mind. It was. But it had drifted away into a recessed corner. Hope had taken center stage again.

I parked in front of the house, and we went in. My dad was asleep on the couch with Sugar and Spider tucked in beside him, Birdie was sitting at the dining-room table working on her laptop, and Jack and Aunt Z were nowhere to be seen.

Birdie looked at us, eyebrows raised in question. We both shook our heads.

"Nothing," I said softly.

Not softly enough, apparently, because my dad shifted and sat up enough to dislodge Spider.

He jumped down and came running toward Jayne. "Mama, Spider hungry."

Birdie rolled her eyes. "I just gave them a handful of treats an hour ago."

He put his front paws on Jayne's leg and peered up at her. "Spider loves Chicken Party."

Jayne scooped him up and kissed his face loudly. "Okay, you silly beast, let's go feed you."

She took him to the kitchen while I sat on the loveseat across from my dad.

"No luck, huh?" he asked as he moved Sugar so he could sit up all the way but scratched her under the chin, which ensured she didn't go anywhere.

"No. But Frank sure owns an interesting mix of places."

He nodded. "I appreciate you kids doing that."

Anything for my mom. "How was your night? Anything new here?"

"Nothing yet. And it was uneventful. You both must be exhausted. You've been up all night."

I was starting to feel it. Until that point, adrenaline had kept me going. "I think a hot shower and a few hours of sleep are probably in order."

Jayne walked back out, her gaze on Birdie. "What are you working on?"

"Nothing." She sighed at the screen. "Just

waiting to see if anything new pops up. What's new with you?"

Jayne shrugged. "Got a text from my dad that he'd have our next store for us soon."

"Maybe it'll be Nocturne Falls," Birdie said. She yawned.

"I doubt it," I said. Then I gave her a little smile. "Thanks for all your hard work, Birdie." Her diligence was amazing. "Have you been up all night too?"

"No, only since about an hour ago. Jack's still sleeping though."

"And Aunt Zinnia's in one of the guest rooms," my dad added. "She's not taking the news about Lila very well. She called every psychic friend she has asking for help."

That sounded promising. "And?"

"Nothing worth following up." My dad got to his feet. He seemed his age to me in that moment. I didn't like it. He glanced at me, then Jayne. "Go rest, the both of you. There are plenty of guest rooms. If anything happens, we'll wake you up."

I stood, and Jayne came over to put her arm around me. "He's right. We should get some sleep."

"I know." As reluctant as I was to sleep, the lack of it was already making me punchy. "Don't let us sleep long."

My dad raised his hand in acknowledgment on the way into the kitchen.

Then a new thought hit me. "Dad?"

He turned. "Yes?"

"Maybe you should call Tony. He said he was going to let you know if he heard anything, but now that he knows what's going on and knows that we suspect Frank... I just think you should talk to him and see how he acts now that he's had a chance to process all this new information."

My dad seemed to mull that over. "You think he was lying to us?"

"No. But my gut says he's involved in this in some way. He might not even realize it yet. A lot could have happened in the few hours that have passed since we saw him. An employee could have said something. He could have heard more from Frank. Who knows?"

Jayne nodded. "Yeah, that's not a bad idea. Kind of take his temperature on this whole thing again."

"All right, I'll do that, but it's a little early. You know the kind of hours show people usually keep. Let's give him a chance to wake up. I don't want him hanging up on me because I called him before sunrise."

The sun was up but just barely, and I understood what my father was saying. Plus my dad probably wanted a cup of coffee to wake himself up a little more. "Right. Makes sense. We'll be in the blue room. Unless Jack or Aunt Z have already claimed it."

"No, that one's free."

I took Jayne's hand, finding comfort in that connection, and we walked back to the guest room. One of many guest rooms in my parents' house, the blue room was decorated in tones of deep blue and gold. It had a kind of postmodern galaxy theme going on that I'd always found restful.

I think the room could have been decorated in neon colors, though, for all the difference it made. We lay down on the bed, fully clothed, and fell asleep in seconds.

If I dreamed, I didn't remember it. And maybe that was for the better because I'm not sure what kind of dreams I would have had, all things considered.

I woke to Jayne's arm across my chest and Sugar on my pillow. I shifted slightly, which was all I could do, being pinned like that, and was about to go back to sleep when I heard conversation in the other room. I couldn't quite make out the words, but it sounded like Birdie and my dad.

The clock said we'd only been asleep for a little over two hours, but I was instantly awake.

I slipped free of Jayne's arm without waking her and got up. Sugar spread out to take up the pillow real estate I'd left behind.

I went out to the living room. I was done sleeping, but I was definitely going to need some coffee. Forget some. A lot of coffee. My dad was standing behind Birdie, and both of them were peering at her computer screen. "Something happening?"

My dad looked over. "Sorry. Didn't mean to wake you. Birdie was just saying the autopsy report was in."

"Autopsy? On… Lou? Already?"

Birdie nodded. "Yes. I guess they didn't have much else going on."

"I know autopsies aren't done in the case where the reason for death was ruled natural causes, so how did you swing it?"

"You're right. They're not," she said. "Unless a family relative requests one or there's an ongoing police matter that involves the decedent."

"You got one of Lou's family members to ask for an autopsy? You are good, Birdie."

She pursed her lips. "Not exactly."

"So how did you get one done?" I really needed coffee.

"I may have pretended to be Lou's sister." She shrugged. "Proof for that sort of thing is pretty easy to whip up online. It's not like they do a lot of checking either."

Jayne walked up beside me. "Checking on what?" She yawned.

"On Birdie pretending to be Lou's sister to get an autopsy report done."

Jayne nodded. "Good job, Birdie. When do you think the report will be in?"

"It just showed up. I was about to read it. It'll take me a few minutes to process it, though. Lots of medical terms and whatnot. Plus there's all the boring stuff to wade through. Age, weight, height, description of the clothing he had on, property he had on him like the contents of his wallet, any personal effects, any scars or tattoos…" She shrugged. "Like I said, I need a few minutes."

"Cool. While you do that, I'm going to get some coffee." She looked at me. "Please tell me there's coffee."

"No idea. I just woke up myself. If there's not coffee, we'll make some, because that's the only way I'm going to stay awake."

My father nodded at the kitchen. "There's plenty. Help yourselves. And if you empty the pot, I'll get another one going."

"Thanks." Jayne headed in.

I lingered a second longer. "Did you call Tony?"

"No, but I guess it's late enough that I can do that now." He took out his phone.

I went after Jayne, desperate for caffeine.

We both filled our cups, and there was still another cup in the pot. I could see us drinking that pretty quickly, though.

"Tony? It's Anson. Sorry for the early hour." In the other room, my dad nodded. "No, nothing yet. That's why I'm calling. Just to see if—oh, sure. I understand. Thanks, though. Right. Talk to you later." He hung up and looked at us, shaking his head. "Nothing new."

"Still worth a shot," I said. "And you didn't wake him so that was good."

"No, he was driving actually. Said Gabi called and was desperate to see him, so he's headed out there. I'm happy for them. That they're working things out." Nothing about my dad said he was happy, but I didn't expect him to be jumping for joy.

Tony might be getting things back on track with his wife, but that only had to make my dad's situation harder.

He came into the kitchen. "Let me make some more. Birdie, you want the last cup before I make a new pot?"

I moved out of his way. I understood needing something to do.

"Sure," she said. She was laser-focused on the PDF document before her. I could just make out an anatomical drawing with notes.

My dad took the pot out to her and refilled her cup. I knew her well enough to know she was going to want cream, sugar, caramel syrup, whipped cream, and a sprinkling of cinnamon, if she could get it.

Except she picked up the cup and took a sip like she always drank black coffee. I straightened. There had to be something pretty interesting in that report for Birdie not to be bothered by a boring cup of joe.

Chapter Twenty-eight

Jayne

I nudged Sinclair. "Are you seeing that?"

"You mean Birdie drinking black coffee?"

I nodded. "That's not normal." Birdie's idea of coffee was that it was a vehicle for sugar and flavorings. The more the merrier.

"No, it's not," Sin said.

"Something's up."

His eyes narrowed slightly. "Agreed."

Simultaneously, we took our coffee into the other room to be closer to her. We sat across from her at the dining-room table, sipping our drinks and waiting with the kind of anticipation I hadn't felt since our wedding day.

We watched her reading. Her gaze stayed fixed on the document, the computer screen lighting up her glasses with a blue glow that made it harder to see her eyes.

She put her hand on her chin, then tapped her upper lip with one finger. "This is interesting."

We both leaned forward and said, "What?"

She didn't look up, just reread something. "They found trace amounts of ketamine in Lou's blood."

"What's that?" I asked. It sounded like a vitamin.

She finally lifted her head. "It's a tranquilizer of sorts."

Sin seemed less impressed. "He was taking a bunch of meds. Wouldn't surprise me if he was taking a few other things that weren't prescribed."

Birdie made a face. "I don't think...let me back up."

Anson came in. "Did you find something?"

"Ketamine," I said, still not totally clear on why that was a big deal yet. "Birdie was about to explain."

He leaned on the back of the couch to listen.

"Ketamine," she started again, "is, well, for one thing, it isn't really prescribed for humans anymore. When it is used, it's generally used as a recreational drug. However, one of the interesting things about ketamine is the way the body metabolizes it. So in Lou's case, the amount that was detected in his system is probably about two percent of what the real dose was. And given that he lived about five hours after you two found him..."

She glanced upward, like she was trying to figure

something out. "My conclusion is that the real dose was far more than anyone would use recreationally." She focused on the screen again, scanning the document before her with more intensity than the last time.

Suddenly, she looked up again. "Did you know he was also a diabetic? The man was not in good health. Overweight, bad heart, high cholesterol." She shook her head. "Whoever did this knew him. Knew what kind of shape he was in."

I couldn't take it. "Did what to him?"

The gleam in her eyes told me she was about to give us the nugget we'd been waiting for. "The ME noted the puncture marks, but Lou was a diabetic, so none of those raised any red flags. And the ketamine wouldn't have been noticed at all if I hadn't asked for the autopsy."

She paused. "I'm ninety-nine percent sure that someone injected him with a large amount of ketamine, which sent him into a state of hypoglycemia that no doubt contributed to his already strained heart being overstressed until it quit."

Sin's dad stopped leaning. "Lou was murdered?"

She nodded. "Looks very much like it."

"Who would do that?" Sin asked. "And why? Tony was about to leave him, so there's no motive there."

I was fixated on the drug itself. "Birdie, who would have access to ketamine? You said it's not used for humans anymore. Would someone have to be a doctor to get it?"

"Not necessarily. It is a club drug. Maybe not the most popular one, but this is Vegas, and there are a lot of clubs in this town. I'm guessing you can pretty much get anything you want to around here."

Anson nodded. "Sad but true."

"So that's it? Anyone could have gotten some?" I shook my head. "That's not helpful."

"Well, it's also an anesthetic and a pain reliever, but it has some hallucinogenic qualities too. That's what makes it a popular recreational drug. However, its most common uses these days are in the veterinarian field. It's used in all kinds of animals. From cats to horses."

I sighed. "Did Lou make a veterinarian mad?"

"Who would want to kill Lou?" Anson shook his head. "It makes no sense."

Jack and Aunt Zinnia came in. Both looked a little perplexed by the conversation, but neither said a word. Jack went into the kitchen, presumably for coffee. Aunt Zinnia followed behind him but got a green juice from the fridge.

Birdie sat back. "There are a lot of reasons for killing someone. This was premeditated, so that eliminates some of them, like a crime of passion. Most likely he knew something someone was afraid might get out."

Things started to click in my brain. "Tony was

supposed to have lunch with Lou the same day he died. Not long after you guys found him."

More of what Birdie had said filtered into my thought process. I stood up, too antsy to sit, and began to walk around the room. "Cats to horses," I repeated.

I'd been in Lou's house and Carrie's house. Neither one had had a cat. And there'd been no cat hair on any of Tony's stuff. I noticed that kind of thing. No sign he'd had a cat from the outside of his house either.

That left horses. Or some other animal.

It hit me like a bolt of lightning. I stopped walking in front of Anson. "Son of a nutcracker. I know where Lila is. I know who has her. And I'm pretty sure Tony's going to be the next one murdered."

Sin jumped up. "Where? Who?"

I turned to face him. "She's at the ranch that Tony owns. Remember he said Gabrielle was staying out there? He specifically said a ranch."

"Right, but I thought we decided Tony wasn't the one who'd taken my mom?"

Birdie was tapping away at her keyboard.

"He isn't." I took a moment, trying to keep my words from jumbling up. "Gabrielle is. But she's been working really hard to make Tony look guilty. The cologne, the Crystal Palace stationery, the pasta."

Sin put a hand on his head like it had all just

become obvious. "And Gabrielle used to work at the Oasis."

I thought back to the article I'd read. "That's right. *A Pussycat in Paris* was the Oasis's last showgirl review."

"As the principal dancer, she'd have to know about the secret tunnel," Sin said. "But I still don't get why she'd kill Lou?"

"He must have found out what she was up to. Tony told us Lou was instrumental in getting them back together. Which means Lou and Gabrielle had to have been in contact recently. Maybe so recently that Lou figured out she'd kidnapped your mom. And Tony was supposed to meet with Lou the same day he died, remember?" I glanced at Anson, who nodded. "She must have visited Lou at his office and jabbed him with a syringe full of ketamine in the hopes of keeping him from telling Tony what she was up to. She might not have meant to kill him. Was there any sign of struggle?"

"No," Anson said. "But why would there have been? He knew her. And considered her a friend."

Birdie was typing away like mad on her laptop.

Sin made a disgusted noise. "Her photo hung in his home office."

I nodded. "And don't ranches have horses?"

"Yes." Birdie sucked in a breath. "Good job, Jayne."

"I know for a fact Tony has horses out there. The day he bought Crimson Dancer, he practically issued a press release announcing he owned the winningest horse in the United States." Anson's eyes were wide. "Tony's headed for the ranch right now. Said Gabrielle asked him to come. That she was desperate to see him."

Birdie looked up from her laptop. "Gabrielle's maiden name is Fine. The screenname of the person Xavier bought the magic book from, the book that started all this, was Superfine. That can't just be a coincidence." She got up. "We need to go now."

"I don't know why Gabi would kidnap Lila, but I'm convinced," Anson said. "Two cars. Birdie and Jack in one, Sin, Jayne, and me in another. Aunt Z, you'd best stay here."

She nodded. "Yes, of course. Be safe. And bring our Lila home."

Anson was already headed for the door. "We will."

We didn't drive so much as speed. We were in Anson's Maserati sedan while Jack and Birdie followed in their rental car. Thankfully, it was still early, and traffic was fairly light.

Anson tried to reach Tony three times, but every time it went to voice mail. "She must have him on the phone to keep him from talking to anyone else. Because there's no way he's there yet."

Anson glanced at the time. "Although he could be, I guess. I don't know when he left." He shook his head. "I bet that book Gabrielle sold to Xavier came from Tony's library. Probably one more way of getting her screws into him. He'd never have given up a book like that on purpose."

Nerves made me chew my bottom lip. "I bet she's not really pregnant. I bet she found out about Tony's affair with Carrie and decided enough was enough."

Sin glanced over his shoulder at me. "But why kidnap my mom?"

I leaned forward a bit. "Because she was an easy way to make Tony look guilty. It's a known fact that he's envious of *Dead Sexy's* success. That he'd love to be the headliner at the Oasis, right?"

"Right," Anson said.

"Look," I continued. "It worked. We thought Tony was behind it. Making your parents breach their contract really seemed like something he'd love to see happen. She probably figured the police would hound him for a few days, ruin his life and reputation and then she'd return Lila, having gotten her revenge on her cheating husband."

"Of course," Sin said. "Gabrielle couldn't have known that my mom was a zombie and that my dad couldn't call the cops because of that."

I took a breath. "She may know now."

Anson looked at me through the rearview mirror. "You really think she's going to kill Tony?"

I nodded, unable to keep the sadness off my face. Tony wasn't the only one I thought she was going to kill.

243

He stared at me. "What else aren't you saying?"

I sighed. "I don't want to put it into words."

His voice was gruff and edged with emotion. "You think she's going to kill Lila too."

I nodded once, then looked out the window. "A murder-suicide would be the ultimate way to get her revenge on Tony. And she's already on the hook for Lou. Why stop now?"

Sin went pale. He glanced at his father. "Drive faster."

Chapter Twenty-nine

Sinclair

My dad parked as close as he could without bringing attention to us, which wasn't very close since the main house had a pretty good view of the drive.

As a result, we parked along a dirt service road that was partially blocked from the house by one of the barns. The land didn't provide much in the way of cover, as it was mostly scrub and rocks with a few scraggly pines here and there. Beautiful country, but my mind wasn't on the scenery.

Jack and Birdie parked behind us and got out. Jack glanced toward the ranch in the distance. "You want us to shift and get out there now or stay with you?"

"Shift and go," my dad said. "Do some recon for us. We need to keep Tony alive, and we need to find Lila. Phones on vibrate."

"You got it," Birdie said.

A moment later, she and Jack shifted and took off toward the ranch, a lone wolf and a raven traveling much faster than we could.

We followed behind them with a decent amount of speed. I was happy my dad's stage time kept him in such good shape. We reached the barn in a few minutes and flattened ourselves against the wall.

My dad shoved a hand into his pocket and took out his phone. "Birdie says Gabrielle has Tony at gunpoint in the living room. Jack is still searching for Lila."

He looked at me. "I'm going to look for your mother too. Can you and Jayne handle Gabrielle?"

I nodded. "With her magic? Easily."

Jayne made a face. "Except if I use magic, I'm exposing myself to humans as a winter elf. I'm not supposed to do that. Don't you think we can just take her out with brute strength and logic?"

"Maybe," my father said. "If you have the element of surprise on your side. But if Gabi kills Tony before you can stop her, Sin, do your thing and get a confession out of him. And make sure you get it on video."

Jayne's brows bent. "But if she kills him before—oh. Never mind."

I grabbed her hand, and we started for the house while my dad went off in another direction. The ranch was huge. Acres and acres of property and numerous outbuildings that included barns, stables, storage sheds, at least one guest house, and a detached garage. There was no telling where my mother might be.

We reached the side of the house and made our way toward the back, but the house was large and sprawling and that took a minute, especially while we were trying to be quiet. There was no sign of Birdie. Maybe she'd gone off to look for my mom too. Thankfully, none of the deck boards creaked as we crept closer to the French doors.

I tried one door as carefully as I could. Locked. I tipped my head toward it, indicating Jayne would have to slip through. I could hear Gabi in the other room, yelling at Tony. We needed to hurry.

Jayne nodded, then disappeared in a wisp of vapor. A moment later, she reappeared and, although a little wobbly, managed to turn the lock.

She braced herself on something out of sight. I eased the door open and left it that way in case anyone needed to get in behind us.

Gabi's voice was rising. "You're not getting out of this."

"Honey, please." Tony's response was much calmer, with a hint of pleading. "I know I screwed up. Bad. But I love you. And I know you love me. And I promise things will be different this time."

Gabi laughed. "Oh, they're going to be different all right. Because you're going to be dead. And everyone's going to think you're a murderer, too."

"Wouldn't it be better to leave him alive to face whatever punishment he's due?"

Jayne and I looked at each other and froze. That was Birdie's voice.

"Shut up," Gabi snapped. "I still haven't decided what to do with you, but you're a trespasser, and trespassers get shot around here. Remember that."

"You need to put that gun down and let me and Tony go," Birdie snapped back. "Or the only thing you're going to remember is being torn apart by a wolf."

We couldn't wait any longer. I pointed at Jayne, then back outside and mouthed the word help.

She nodded and slipped away. Hopefully, she'd return shortly with my dad and Jack. Or at least one of them.

I walked into the living room with my hands up, my voice calm, and what I hoped was a nonthreatening style.

Gabi glanced at me, a little wild-eyed. The gun remained pointed at Tony and Birdie.

"Hi, Gabrielle. I'm Sinclair Crowe. Anson and Lila's son." Decent start, but I wasn't exactly an expert in talking down women with guns intent on killing their cheating husbands. "How about we all take a beat and work this out without that gun? You don't really want to kill Tony, do you? Is he worth you going to jail over?"

Of course, she was already going to jail because of Lou, but there was no point in reminding her about that.

She glared at me. Her hand was remarkably steady holding that gun. I guessed her years on stage had taught her how to deal with nerves. "I absolutely do want to kill him. And I'm sorry about your mother, but she has to die too."

I needed a moment after that statement, then I found my words. "Why is that?" I gave myself points for not letting my anger show through.

"Because I need to frame Tony so that he's not some martyr. Her death is what's going to keep me from going to jail. See, I will have caught Tony in the act of killing her, and as I try to stop him and grab the gun, he's going to end up getting shot."

Birdie snorted. "Forensics will see right through that."

"Shut up," Gabi yelled.

And just like that, we were back to level five crazy. I knew Birdie didn't intend to stir the pot, but I had to take us from a boil to a simmer once again. "Gabi? Can I call you Gabi? It's not the best plan I've ever heard." I held my hand out, palm up. "Why don't you give me the gun, and we can figure something else out. The pregnancy hormones have to be tough. They can't be helping right now, are they? I'm sure the police would be understanding about that."

They probably wouldn't, but it sounded good.

Gabi frowned at me. "I'm not pregnant. I just told Tony that to get him to come back to me. And speaking of police, why didn't you and your father call them when your mother went missing? Don't you care about her?"

That was a little harder to answer. "We care very much. We love her beyond words. We didn't call the police because…"

"I'm a psychic, and I told them not to," Birdie said.

I jumped on board that train immediately. "That's right. She's our family psychic. She led us here, too." In for a penny, in for a pound.

Gabi actually seemed to be considering that information. Wasn't that surprising, really. Lots of people, not just in this town, were superstitious and prone to suggestions. It was one of the reasons hypnotist shows were so popular and had no shortage of willing participants.

Gabi gave Birdie a more thorough stare-down. I think the blue hair and the bedazzled T-shirt helped sell the psychic angle even more. But then Gabi had lived in Vegas a long time. Her skepticism of such things had to be pretty high.

Birdie seemed to sense that and apparently decided to lean into the role a little more. "The people who are most open to being helped by my gifts can see my psychic ability in my eyes."

"Is that so?" Now Gabi's skepticism was coming through loud and clear. "I don't see anything."

Birdie pushed her glasses up on top of her head. "Look again."

The faintest wolfy glow lit Birdie's gaze.

Tony jerked back as he let out a soft curse, clearly amazed.

Gabi's mouth was open and her eyes rounded, but she didn't say anything. Just stared. She lowered the gun slightly. Finally, she gave Birdie a nod. "If you're so psychic, tell me something no one else would know."

Birdie closed her eyes and held her hand out toward Gabi. A second later, she opened her eyes. The wolfy glow was in full effect. "You've already killed someone. A man close to you." She glanced at Tony. "A man close to both of you."

Gabi's gaze went wide.

"Lou?" Tony whispered. He stared at his wife. "You killed Lou?"

"I didn't mean to," Gabi said. She looked a little panicked now. She stared at Birdie again. "All right, psychic. How does this end?"

Birdie, now fully absorbed by the idea that she could predict the future, stretched her arms out and tipped her head back a little. Maybe she was feeling for the spirits? I wasn't sure. But her showmanship was working. Light glittered off her T-shirt's embellishments. After a moment, she shook her head.

"Not well, I'm afraid."

"What do you mean?" Gabi asked. The gun dropped a few inches more.

Birdie put her fingers to her temples. "If Tony dies…you end up in prison for the rest of your life. If Tony lives…" She sighed and waved one hand at the gun. "There is too much uncertainty for me to predict clearly what becomes of you with all that metal interfering with the cosmic frequencies."

Gabi's eyes narrowed, and she brought the gun back up sharply. "You're lying. I don't know how you did the eye trick, but my soon-to-be-dead husband makes people believe all kinds of magic are possible."

Birdie protested. "That was no trick. That was—"

"For the last time, shut up." Gabi cocked the weapon. "Looks like I'm just going to have to kill all of you."

Chapter Thirty

Jayne

I ran straight back to the last place I'd seen Anson. The barn. I pulled the door open and immediately found him. No sign of Lila, however. "Hey, we need your help at the house. Gabi's got—"

He wasn't looking at me but behind me. I turned to see an older man in jeans and a work shirt pointing a rifle at us. He had the lean, rangy look of a ranch hand.

"Jayne," Anson began. "This is Buck Murphy."

Or a stagehand. Snowballs. I had a strong feeling he hadn't won that deposited money gambling so much as he'd gotten it from Gabrielle for his help. That also explained how Gabrielle had known the show's timing and when to nab Lila. Maybe he'd even been the one to tip Lou off about Lila's disappearance.

Buck gestured with the rifle. "Get over there with Crowe."

I moved closer to Anson, putting my hands up. "Hey, we're not armed. We're not going to hurt you."

He sneered at me. "Think you're pretty smart, don't you? Figured out the money, huh?"

"No, actually," I said. "Well, we found out about the money. But we thought you'd won that at the blackjack table. It was Gabrielle who gave it all away. She killed Lou Scholtz with a big dose of ketamine. And she was the only one connected to this whole thing with easy access to the drug."

"That stupid…" Buck shook his head.

I needed to know more. "Was Lou going to spill the beans? Is that why she killed him?"

"She didn't mean to kill him. Just knock him out until she could wrap things up." Buck nodded. "He came out to the ranch and saw her moving Lila into the small barn."

Beside me, Anson tensed. "Is that where Lila is?"

Buck scoffed, his grip on the rifle tightening. "Not anymore."

I did my best to distract him. "Lou must have told her what? That he was going to tell Tony? That she had to make things right?"

"He told her she had until the next afternoon to get Lila home and everything smoothed out or he'd tell Tony. Lou's problem was he always had a soft spot for Gabrielle. Anyone else would have called the police right away. But she cried and made eyes at him and told him she just wanted Tony to appreciate her or some crap like that."

I nodded. "You could still get out of this unscathed, you know. Anson and I would be totally willing to look the other way if you'd just let us go." I nudged him. "Wouldn't we?"

Anson nodded quickly. "I'd even let you keep your job."

Buck frowned. "You would?"

"Sure. If you're willing to be a team player, why shouldn't I reward that?" Anson was inching closer to me for some reason. I figured I'd know soon enough. "Let us go, help us find Lila, and this will all be forgotten."

Buck seemed to be considering that, which probably meant he was dumber than he looked.

Anson pressed his arm into my elbow and whispered, "Don't freak out."

A second later I felt like I was falling through some kind of space-time vortex. Everything whirled around me in streaks of light and movement.

In a flash, it was over. Anson and I were standing outside of the barn. About where we'd been earlier. He'd conjured us away.

Inside, Buck was shouting. Mostly about where had we gone and he was going to get us.

"Can you seal the doors shut with ice?" Anson asked. "Keep him in there?"

"Heck, yes." There were wide doors on both sides, I imagined so tractors or trucks could be driven inside. I lifted my hands and sealed the one on our side with a thick coating of ice all around the seams. "Oof. This is taking more work than usual. Not much water in the air around here."

"Will you be able to do the other side?"

"Yes." Whatever it took, I'd get it done. "Let's go."

We ran around to the other set of doors. Buck was just sliding them back. Anson shoved them shut again, which caused Buck to do more yelling.

While Anson held the doors in place, I sealed them. The drain was instant. I felt like I could lie down and nap.

Then a loud pop broke the desert's calm.

Anson looked instantly panicked. He shifted toward the house, where the sound had come from.

I swallowed. "Tell me that wasn't a gunshot."

He didn't answer, just took off running. I was right behind him. Jack came out from one of the storage sheds, saw us, and yelled, "House?"

We both nodded. That got him running too.

I'd left the French doors open, something I was very glad about because it was one less obstacle in our way.

We burst into the house.

"Sin? Are you okay?"

"Yes, in here."

We came around into the living room, and Jack

let out a strangled cry. Birdie was on the floor, blood all over her arm and shoulder.

He rushed to her. "Birdie."

She smiled weakly up at him. "It's just a flesh wound. And Sin already called 911. Took the breath out of me, though."

Tony had the gun and was holding it on Gabrielle, who looked like she very much wanted it back so she could use it.

I went down to my knees beside Birdie, taking the hand Jack wasn't already holding. "What happened?"

Sin filled me in. "Gabi took a shot at Tony—"

"He insulted me," Gabi snarled.

Tony gruffed out a breath. "I said you were crazy. It's only an insult if it's not true."

"Enough," Sin growled.

They shut up.

Sin finished. "Birdie went to shove him out of the way, and the bullet grazed her shoulder."

I exhaled. That didn't seem so bad.

"Ruined my good T-shirt," Birdie sniped.

I laughed to keep from crying. "I'll buy you another one."

Sin looked at his dad. "Have you found mom yet?"

"No," he said softly.

I'd had about as much as I could take. I patted Birdie's hand. "I'll be right back. It's time to end this." Then I pushed to my feet, walked over to

Gabrielle, and grabbed her by the throat, lifting her off the ground enough so that only her toes touched the floor. "Where's Lila?"

She snorted and sputtered. "Get your hands off me, you—"

I pushed a sharp wave of cold through my body and into hers via my hand.

Her words disappeared in a shuddering breath. "I'm so c-cold."

"And going to get colder if I don't get an answer now." To underline my point, I took her down a few more degrees.

Her eyes bulged. "W-wine c-cellar."

"Where is that? Downstairs?" She didn't answer me. I looked at Anson. "I thought houses in Vegas didn't have basements?"

"Most don't," he answered. "But it's a little easier to dig them in the desert."

Tony gestured with his free hand. "Back through the kitchen. Glass and iron door."

"Sin, go with your dad. We've got this." I glared at Gabi. "Because you're certainly not going to try anything, are you?"

She tried to shake her head, but she was shivering too hard. I eased up on the cooldown as Sin and Anson took off for the lower part of the house.

The soft cry of sirens filled the air. In that moment, they were the most beautiful sound I'd ever heard.

258

Chapter Thirty-one

Sinclair

My father and I raced through the kitchen, found the glass and iron door, whipped it open, and plunged down the stairs in the dark.

"Lila, can you hear me? Lila?" My father called for her, but there was no answer.

I found a light switch and flipped it. No mom but rack after rack of wine bottles lined the walls. In the center was a plush little seating area. Very posh, but I couldn't have cared less.

"There." My dad pointed to a small room at the end with another wrought-iron and glass door. "Has to be."

He ran to the door, nodding immediately. "She's in there. And she doesn't look good." He tried the door, but it was locked. He stepped back, turned his body toward the door, and rammed it with his shoulder.

This wasn't the time for the subtleties of magic.

I joined him as the glass shattered and the metal groaned. He reached through the debris to unlock the door and finally got it open. "Lila, honey, I'm here."

My mother was tied to a chair in the center of the small room, her head slumped to one side, a gag in her mouth. I was going to kill Gabi. I went to work getting the gag off my mom while my dad untied her arms and legs.

He talked softly to her the whole time. "I'm here, sweetheart. So is Sinclair. We've got you now, and we're going to take you home. You're going to be all right."

She mumbled something I couldn't make out. She was in terrible shape. Her skin was dry and cracked and flaking off in big pieces. The circles under her eyes looked like bruises, and her cheeks were sunken in. I knew her regime of moisturizers and vitamins was important to her, but I never realized just how much.

And this was after barely two days.

I didn't know how my father was holding it together. I was so angry, I was shaking. The only solace was that Gabrielle was going to pay for this. So would anyone else involved.

We got her untied just as sounds filled the house above us. The EMTs had arrived.

"Anson," she whispered.

He picked her up in his arms, cradling her against his chest. "I'm here, baby. We're going home."

"How are we going to explain this?" I glanced upward, desperate to protect my mother from any more injury or insult. "The EMTs are going to wonder what's going on with her. Why she looks like this."

He hesitated. "They don't need to know she was here. I'll take her out the back. Straight to the car and straight home. I'll call Dr. Brewer on the way. You and Jayne can go with Jack and Birdie."

I nodded. Dr. Brewer was a witch and handled a lot of supernatural clients. She'd been my parents' doctor for years. Mine too, when I lived with them. "Good. Get her out of here." I grabbed her hand, leaned in, and kissed her cheek. "I love you, mom."

She managed a tiny half-smile. "Love you, too, Sin."

I looked at my dad again. "Let me go up first. Make sure it's clear."

"Okay."

I jogged up the steps. There was no one in the kitchen, so I gave him a nod. "All good."

As they left, I went back to the living room. The EMTs were at Birdie's side, dealing with her flesh wound. Jayne and Jack had taken a step back to give them room to work, and Tony still had Gabrielle at gunpoint.

The front door was open, and the exterior of the

house was lit up like a carnival with all the flashing lights. And it was about to get more interesting. Two cops were walking toward the front door, guns drawn. This wasn't giving me a good feeling. I glanced at Jayne. But we were out of time.

One of the cops aimed his gun at Tony. "Sir, put the weapon down."

Jayne and I both lifted our hands.

Tony glanced over his shoulder, saw the police, and dropped the gun, then raised his hands as well. "This woman is my wife. Gabrielle. She shot the woman on the floor." He looked at me, as if asking whether or not he should say anything about my mother.

I gave a quick shake of my head. Gabrielle should already do a good stretch of time for shooting at Birdie and killing Lou. Charging her with my mother's kidnapping would have been a nice addition, but involving my mother would mean exposing her true nature.

Keeping her secret was the whole reason my father had slipped away with her.

And while I realized Tony didn't understand any of that, he clearly knew we didn't want the press for our own reasons. I appreciated that. He might be a man of questionable character, but at least in this instance, he'd made a good choice.

Or had he? The more I thought about it, the more I realized we could be in trouble if we left my mom out of this. I muttered a few choice words, then dove in. "This woman also kidnapped my mother, Lila Crowe. My father, Anson Crowe, has already taken her home."

The second cop frowned. "Your parents are the Vegas performers?"

"Yes, and the man who just dropped the gun is Tony Tortellini. Another Vegas performer."

The cop kept frowning. "Your father shouldn't have entered a crime scene."

"My mother was tied to a chair and gagged. You can see the evidence of that pretty plainly if you go down to the wine cellar. I'm sure you'll also find her fingerprints, as well as mine, my father's, and Gabrielle's. That should help, right?" What they'd make of the skin flakes, I had no idea.

"Yes, but—"

"She was scared, dehydrated and in need of rest. You can contact my parents if you need a further statement. I'll make sure you have their information."

That seemed to mollify the officer. At least temporarily. Thankfully, I knew that in general, Vegas didn't allow too much bad press to get out. One performer kidnapping another performer would definitely be considered bad press. Vegas was all about protecting the brand.

I guess what happened in Vegas really did stay in Vegas.

I knew there would still be paperwork and

questions, but hopefully, it could all be handled without my mom's secret being revealed.

How the rest of this turned out remained to be seen. The EMTs, whether they realized it or not yet, were working on a werewolf. There was every chance this could still become a very tricky situation.

An hour later, Tony and Gabrielle were in separate squad cars, about to be taken in for questioning. Gabrielle was in handcuffs. Tony was not.

Jayne, Jack, and I had been asked to step outside so the EMTs could finish dressing Birdie's wound. We'd all spoken to the cops. Jayne had told them about Buck, who I was surprised to find out about, and Jack had left to move the other car closer to the front of the house in preparation for taking Birdie home.

I checked my phone again, but there was still no word from my father. They should have gotten home about twenty minutes ago, but I also knew he'd be occupied with taking care of my mom and explaining what had happened to Dr. Brewer. None of that kept me from wanting a quick status update.

I'd never seen my mother look that close to death, and it had shaken me.

While we stood there, another pair of squad cars arrived.

I watched them as I spoke to Jayne. "If they're here for Buck, you'd better get that ice off the barn."

"But he'll escape."

"Only if he realizes the doors aren't frozen shut anymore. And if he does, they can put out an APB on him. It's better than explaining how that ice got there."

"True." She took hold of my arm and leaned on me, then a few seconds later announced, "It's gone. Much easier than creating it, I can tell you that."

The cops approached us. "Can one of you direct us to the barn where the second suspect is being detained?"

"I'll take you," I said. I looked at Jayne. "You stay here in case Birdie needs you."

She nodded. "Okay."

"Right this way, officers." I led them toward the barn with no intention of going farther than necessary.

"You're the son of the woman who was kidnapped?" the female officer asked me.

"Yes, that's right."

She smiled and nodded. "I saw your parents' show last year. My husband took me for our anniversary. Best show I've ever seen."

"Thank you." I stopped us behind one of the storage sheds. "The barn on the other side of this is where you'll find Buck Murphy. Provided he's still in there. He was one of my father's stagehands, and he helped Gabrielle Tortellini coordinate the kidnapping of my mother. She paid him a considerable sum to do it."

Both cops pulled their weapons. "Go back to the house now, sir. We'll handle it from here."

"Thanks." I started for the house. The sooner we could be home, the better. I wanted all of this behind us. That thought stopped me and turned me toward the officers again. They were just about to make their approach. "Are we free to go?"

The female officer nodded without looking at me. "We have your contact information. Now please, get clear of the area."

I didn't need to be told twice. Without another word, I ran for the house. Jayne was standing in the yard right where I'd left her, and Jack was back at her side. She had her arms wrapped around her body like she was giving herself a hug, and she didn't look too happy. I hoped nothing bad had happened. Then I heard the shouting from inside the house. "What's going on?"

"They want to transport Birdie by ambulance to the hospital. Birdie, on the other hand, wants to go home."

Jack shook his head. "I already know who's going to win."

I nodded. "Yep."

Right on cue, the EMTs walked out with the police officers behind them. Another second and Birdie appeared at the door, arm in a sling.

The EMTs looked like they'd had enough and

were happy to leave. The officers seemed amused about something.

We all looked at Birdie.

"Don't just stand there," she said. "Help me lock this place up so we can leave."

Chapter Thirty-two

Jayne

Sin drove, and I rode up front with him. On the way, Birdie explained how she'd managed a private word with the officer in charge, who also happened to be shifter. Coyote, she told us. After their brief conversation, during which she explained what was really going on, he promised her he'd handle things. Like getting the EMTs out of the way before Birdie's natural healing powers made her wound disappear altogether.

She had the officer's card in her pocket and looked pretty pleased with herself. I didn't blame her. Making that connection would probably save Sin's parents a lot of aggravation.

She fell asleep before we made it to the house.

Sin parked and got the car door for Jack, who carried her in.

"I think they gave her some heavy pain meds," he said. "She'll probably sleep for a while. I'll just take her back to the guest room and stay with her. If you need me, just say the word."

"No problem," Sin said. "We owe her a lot for her help. Anything she needs, you just let us know. And I mean anything."

"Will do." He went off down the hall with her.

I took Sin's hand. "Go see how your mom is. I know you're worried about her. We both are." He hadn't said much about her except to tell me she hadn't looked good when they'd found her.

I could only imagine what that meant.

"Come with me," Sin said.

I shook my head. "No, you go. She probably doesn't want to see anyone but family right now."

"You are family, babe."

I smiled. "I mean you and your dad. Go on. You're wasting time."

He kissed my cheek, then took off.

I walked out into the living room. Aunt Zinnia was in the kitchen making something for dinner. My stomach grumbled, and I realized how little I'd eaten lately. It did smell good in the house but not entirely like dinner.

I leaned on the breakfast bar. "What are you working on?" There were too many ingredients covering the counters and too many bowls and pots filling the sink to tell what was going on.

"Comfort food." She smiled. "Chicken and rice casserole, green beans with bacon, and biscuits for dinner, with chocolate cherry cobbler for dessert."

"That sounds amazing and perfect." The smells made sense now. "Anything I can do to help?"

"Child, you have helped enough already. Thank you for everything you did to get Lila home. This family will forever be indebted to you and your friends."

"This family is my family." Then I shrugged. "There's nothing I wouldn't do to help."

"You're a good girl. I'm so glad you and Sinclair ended up together. And you're right. This family is absolutely your family."

Sugar came tearing through the living room, Spider hot on her heels. They zipped past us, ran around the dining-room table, then back through the living room and disappeared again.

I laughed. "I think they're a little bored. Usually we try to play with them more. And we've been a little preoccupied lately. Not that it could be helped."

"Well, if they keep that up, they'll have to nap soon."

"Do you have any pets?" I couldn't remember if we'd talked about that or not.

"No. The place where I live doesn't allow them." A sly smile bent her fuchsia-tinted lips. "Which is why I've decided to move."

"What?"

She nodded as she sprinkled breadcrumbs over the casserole. "Don't say anything just yet, but I'm going to take Anson and Lila up on their offer to move here with them. As soon as Lila's well enough to handle it, that is. After what just happened…" She shook her head, her voice suddenly thick with emotion. "I just want to be closer, that's all."

"I can totally understand that."

She brushed her hands off. "And once I do, I'm going to get a cat."

Spider jumped up onto the chair next to me, making me jerk back in surprise. He put his front paws on the counter. "Someone say Spider's name?"

"No." I laughed and ruffled the fur on his head. "But we were talking about cats."

Aunt Zinnia made eyes at Spider. "Look at that handsome boy. I hope I can find a looker just like him."

Spider kneaded his paws against the granite counter. "Auntie says Spider handsome."

"Because you are." I booped his nose. "Handsome and full of yourself." I looked at Aunt Zinnia. "Be careful what you wish for."

"Oh, I know Spider is a one-of-a-kind kitty, but I want one with just as much personality. Granted, getting one that talks would be a bonus, but I know that's not going to happen."

"You never know. I mean, we live in a pretty interesting world." I made a mental note to see about getting her one of the prototype translation collars, if she did actually adopt a cat. Sometimes it was good to be a royal who could pull those kinds of strings.

"That is very true." She picked up the enormous casserole. "Could you open the oven for me?"

"Sure." I came around the breakfast bar to do as she'd asked.

Sin walked out looking like he'd been punched in the gut.

Immediately, my stomach sank. I left Zinnia to finish with the food. "What is it?"

He shook his head. "She's not doing well. It's more than just dehydration. Dr. Brewer thinks she needs a blood transfusion to have any chance at a full recovery."

My hand went to my mouth. Worry made me sick. "Can the doctor do that?"

"Yes, but she's got to find the right kind of blood my mom needs."

"I'm O negative. I'm a universal donor."

His lips parted. "You are?"

"Yes. Go see if that will work. We can do it right now."

"Okay." He ran back down the hall.

Aunt Zinnia came over, cupped my face in her hands for a moment, then pulled me into her arms and hugged me. "You're such a good girl."

She was squeezing me so hard, I couldn't quite

get enough breath to answer her properly. "Thanks," I managed.

Sin came back a few seconds later. "Dr. Brewer says that will work."

Aunt Zinnia let me go so she could clap. "Such good news."

I took a deep, welcome breath. "All right. Let's do this."

Within a few minutes, I was lying on the bed next to Lila. It was heartbreaking to see her in such a wretched state. She was almost nonresponsive and looked as if a strong wind would blow her into dust. Her lips were parched, her skin cracked and flaking. Even her nails and hair looked brittle.

I told myself that was all going to change very soon. That thought alone was what kept me from crying.

From Anson's red-rimmed eyes, he'd already been doing that. "Thank you, Jayne."

"I'm happy to help."

Sin stood beside the bed, holding my hand. He looked on the verge of tears himself. I understood. If the situation were reversed and my mom was as sick as Lila, I'd have been a puddle of rage and emotion.

Dr. Brewer came over with her supplies. Her dark hair was pinned into a big, messy bun, and her eye makeup was on point. Something about that was very reassuring. I mean, if she could nail that kind of

273

precision liner application, a little blood transfusion should be a piece of cake.

At the thought of cake, my stomach grumbled again.

"Are you hungry?" Sin asked.

"Apparently." I didn't want to tell him I'd been thinking about cake. But I was definitely going to need sugar after this.

Dr. Brewer smiled at me. "This won't hurt a bit. Just a pinch so I can get the needle in, and then the hard part is over."

I nodded. "Do whatever you need to do." It didn't hurt that she was a witch. I was hoping that meant there'd be a little magical pain reliever.

"I'll need your arm flat on the bed." She looked at Sin. "Sorry. You'll have to let go of her hand."

"Okay." He gave me one last squeeze, then released me.

I put my arm out straight. And closed my eyes. I wasn't that squeamish, but this was still a needle going into my arm for the express purpose of removing my blood.

I guess it was a good thing Greyson and I hadn't worked out.

All vampire ex-boyfriend references aside, I was fine not knowing the details of the transfusion. "Just tell me when it's over."

"Will do," Dr. Brewer said. "If you feel faint, let me know, all right?"

"Yep." I took a few deep breaths. She cleaned my arm with alcohol or something that felt cool on my skin. That one act made what was about to happen all the more real. And it hit me that if my blood didn't help Lila, her last moments might be right here next to me.

I was overwhelmed with grief at the idea.

"Um, sweetheart?" Sin's fingers brushed my palm.

"Yes?"

"It's snowing in the bedroom."

I opened my eyes. Large, fluffy flakes drifted down from the ceiling. "Sorry." I put a stop to that and got my emotions under check. The melodrama could wait until there was reason for it. Right now, I needed to focus on Lila getting well. Positive thoughts and all that.

"Small pinch now," Dr. Brewer said.

"Okay." I winced as the needle went in. More like a medium pinch, but I wasn't going to argue. I pushed out a breath as my stomach turned over from nerves.

"Lila, small pinch now," I heard Dr. Brewer say from the other side of the bed.

There was no response from Lila. Not a moan, not a sigh, nothing.

I kept my eyes closed. If this didn't work, I was going to cry like a baby. Snowballs. I was probably going to cry regardless.

Sin laid his hand over mine. I was afraid to move too much with the needle in my arm, but I was glad for the contact. Then I felt his hair against my fingers, and I realized he must have kneeled beside the bed and was now resting his head near my hand.

His closeness was comforting but also a reminder of how desperate the situation was. I tried not to think about whether or not I could feel the blood leaving my body, but I couldn't stop myself.

I really could feel it. Sort of.

A soft gasp beside me ended that line of thought.

"Lila, can you hear me?" Dr. Brewer asked. "It's all right. I'm giving you a blood transfusion."

"Cold," Lila whispered.

I opened my eyes. "That's my fault. It's my blood."

"It's okay," Dr. Brewer reassured me. "It's not just you."

What did that mean? Was Lila close to death? I couldn't hold back any longer. Tears slipped down my temples, dampening my hair. "Is she…?"

Sin kissed my fingers, then pressed them to his cheek.

Dr. Brewer glanced over at me, a stethoscope in her ears. She nodded as she took the end of the stethoscope off of Lila's chest. "I believe it's working. I'm just not sure she's going to be a zombie anymore."

Chapter Thirty-three

Sinclair

The two most important women in my life were currently asleep, but they were also healthy. Nothing else mattered. Jayne had saved my mother's life, and while my mom still had some recovering to do, Dr. Brewer felt certain she'd be fine.

And after a few minutes, Dr. Brewer decided my mother probably *would* remain a zombie, but thanks to Jayne's powerfully magic blood, Dr. Brewer thought my mom might not look quite so much like a zombie as she once had.

I was pretty sure my mom would be okay with that.

Dr. Brewer had left once my mother had fallen asleep with the command that we call her if any issues arose, although she doubted they would. Besides rest and pain meds if needed, Dr. Brewer said getting my mom back on her moisturizing and vitamin routines should have her up and around shortly.

I knew my dad was still worried about her. And although he hadn't said it, probably worried about the show. Tomorrow night would be the third night dark. Gabrielle was going to get what she'd been after all along.

They'd officially be in breach of contract. That had to be weighing on him, but I also knew my mother's health was the only thing that really mattered.

The show would find a new home. Maybe not at a place quite as prestigious as the Oasis, but right now, who cared? I glanced down at my wedding ring. Family was what mattered most. Being together.

And my parents had that again.

Aunt Zinnia set the casserole on the table. Birdie had roused a few minutes ago to join Jack, my dad and me at the table.

"That looks wonderful, Zinnia," Birdie said.

"Thank you." Aunt Z took a seat near my father.

Birdie inhaled, nodding. "Food is very important for a shifter's recovery."

"So is sugar."

We all turned to see Jayne shuffling toward us, a smile on her face.

I got up from my chair. "You should be resting."

She slanted her eyes at me with the kind of long-suffering look I'd grown accustomed to. "I gave blood, not a kidney. I'm fine. Actually, I'm starving, and I need to eat something."

"Then you should eat." After what she'd done, I'd go out and buy her doughnuts if that's what she wanted.

"Oh, I'm gonna." She took the seat next to me, looking up at me expectantly.

There was no plate. Grinning at her, I kissed the top of her head and went to get a setting for her. When I came back with the plate and utensils, I put the fork and knife down but filled her plate with a good helping of chicken and rice casserole, a spoonful of green beans with bacon, and a biscuit. "There you go."

After a few bites, Jayne gave Aunt Zinnia a nod. "You're a fantastic cook. This is the best meal I've had in a long time."

"She's right," Birdie said. "Your biscuits are pretty impressive for someone who's not a Southerner."

Aunt Z grinned. "I appreciate that."

Jack sipped his iced tea. "I'm kind of surprised you're not married with this kind of ability."

Aunt Z laughed. "I've had offers. But I'm a very particular woman."

Jayne glanced at me while she buttered the other half of her biscuit. "How's your mom doing?"

"She's still sleeping."

"Good."

My dad put his fork down. "I should go check on her."

"No need, sweetheart. I'm right here."

A collective gasp came up from everyone. My dad got to his feet and rushed to my mother's side.

"Are you okay? I'm not sure you should be up."

I understood his concern, but she looked radiant. There was no other word for it. If someone told me she'd just gotten back from a week at the best spa the desert could offer, I'd have believed them. There were no visible spots of flaking skin, and the normal dark shadows under her eyes and in the hollows of her cheeks seemed a lot less than usual. "You look pretty great, mom. Especially considering how you were before."

"See? Listen to your son." She gave my father a sharp but loving poke in the ribs. "Now don't start babying me. I feel good. A little weak. And also very hungry. Like my daughter-in-law."

Jayne smiled. "Probably a side effect of having winter elf blood in your veins."

With tears in her eyes, my mother walked over to Jayne. "You saved my life."

Jayne stood. "I did what anyone else would have done."

My mom pulled her into a hug. "Thank you." She held on to Jayne, eyes closed, arms tight around her. "I can't say it enough. Thank you."

Jayne just hugged her back, nodding and looking weepy.

After a few more moments, my mom let her go, pulling back so she could look Jayne in the face. "Your blood must be pretty amazing, because I feel stronger than I have in a long time. And I looked in the mirror. None of my moisturizers or vitamins has ever made me look this good. Maybe it'll wear off in few days, maybe it won't, but I don't care. You did a wonderful thing for me."

Jayne sniffed. "I was happy to do it."

"I know you were," my mom said. "Because you are the best daughter-in-law a mother could ever hope for." She smiled brightly. "Now, I am going to *eat*."

She did too. We all did. Having my mom back and in such amazing shape after everything she'd been through was the only seasoning the meal needed.

Aunt Zinnia had made enough for an army, but we went through the food on the table like locusts. At one point, she even floated the idea of making another tray of biscuits.

Jayne put an end to that by reminding everyone that there was still chocolate cherry cobbler to be had.

My father upped the ante with an announcement there was more than enough French vanilla ice cream to go with it.

So by the time dessert rolled around, we had groaning stomachs and high spirits. Laughter and merriment filled the house. Even Spider and Sugar joined us, sitting on the stools at the kitchen counter so they could be at eye level with us.

A few bits of chicken and bacon might have gotten tossed their way, too.

We all retold our stories from the rescue. How Buck held my dad and Jayne at gunpoint in the barn. How Birdie got shot saving Tony. How my dad slipped away with my mom to keep her secret safe. And how Birdie smoothed everything over by befriending the coyote-shifter police officer.

When the meal was done, Aunt Z served up the still-warm cobbler, and then my dad added a scoop of ice cream to each dish.

As we tucked in, making all the appropriate happy noises to such a delicious finish to a great meal, my mother raised her water glass. "Thank you all for what you did to help me. If I spent the rest of my life trying, I couldn't repay you."

"Hear! Hear!" my father said, raising his glass as well.

We all put our glasses in the air and clinked them together.

My mom took a sip, then put her glass down and smiled at my dad. "I can't wait to get back to work tomorrow."

His brows bent, and he smiled at her like she'd

lost her mind. "Sweetheart, that is not going to happen. You need to rest."

"Anson." That tone was the same one that had stopped me in my tracks many times as a child. "I am doing that show with or without you tomorrow. We cannot go dark a third night in a row. You know that."

"Lila, you need to—"

"We're not discussing it," my mom said. "The show is happening. End of the conversation."

Aunt Zinnia stared over my mother's head. "Um...why is it snowing in the living room?"

"Babe," I said to Jayne. "What's up with the flurries?"

She shook her head. "That's not me."

Spider and Sugar jumped down to chase the drifting flakes.

"Mama," Spider said. "Snow fun."

Sugar caught one and ate it. "Cold treats."

Everyone looked at Jayne as the snow continued to fall.

"It's not me," she said. "But..." With a curious grin, she turned to look at my mom. "It might be Lila."

Chapter Thirty-four

Jayne

"That's close. You've almost got it," I told Lila. The men were cleaning up the kitchen after dinner while Zinnia and Birdie were relaxing on the back deck, having a glass of wine.

Lila and I had retreated to the smaller sitting room because I needed to get Lila comfortable with her new skill before it went sideways.

She groaned. "I don't feel like I'm getting it at all."

"Think soft thoughts. I know that sounds weird. Like what's a soft thought? But I promise, that's how my dad taught me."

Her expression darkened a little. "It was easier when I wasn't thinking about it."

I could tell she was getting frustrated with the repeated attempts to master her new winter elf magic, but she was so close, I didn't want to call it quits just yet. Not when she was picking it up this quickly. "I understand, but that was an emotional reaction. That's not a good way to use a skill like this. You don't want to be out shopping, find the perfect little black dress and suddenly there's a blizzard in the mall, right?"

She rolled her eyes, sighing. "Nope, definitely don't want that."

I put my hands on my hips and gave her my best encouraging look. "Don't lose sight of the fact that you've just inherited these skills, and in such a short time of having them, you're doing fantastic."

"If you say so."

"I do say so. And as the first winter zombie, you're doing an incredible job."

She was smiling now. "Okay, here goes again."

A couple of seconds ticked by, and then small, delicate snowflakes began to fall in the sitting room. I watched as the first few reached the terracotta tiles. They touched down and vanished without a trace of dampness left behind.

I pressed my hands together in front of my chest. "You did it!"

"I did?"

I nodded. "Yes, that was perfect. Wow, you're a fast learner. That was amazing."

I never anticipated that my donation of blood to save Lila's life would result in her receiving some of my shimmer powers. So far, making it snow and creating small objects from ice seemed to be the extent of it. I was glad about that. I wasn't sure how my uncle would feel if someone outside the immediate family could do his slide.

Lila raised her hands in the air. "Yes!" She clapped, giving herself a little applause. New snow started to fall. "Thank you for your patience." Then she glanced up. "Oh. I guess I don't have that great a handle on it as I thought."

"That just proves that even though you're handling these new skills so well, you need to keep practicing. A strong burst of emotion still catches me off guard every once in a while. Promise me you'll practice."

"I will. Trust me, if there's anything I understand, it's how necessary practice is for perfecting a skill. Especially one with a magical side."

I nodded. "I have no doubt that's true. It's probably that familiarity that's helping you get the hang of this so quickly." She still looked phenomenal. The transfusion had done wonders for her. But that was all on the outside. "How are you feeling?

"Good. The weakness is already less than it was when I first got up."

I had one more question I had to ask. "Are you nervous about tomorrow's show?"

She hesitated. "A little. After all, the last time I went through that tunnel, things didn't go so well.

I think I'm going to ask Anson about putting a stagehand back there. Just to make sure things run smoothly."

"A stagehand you trust," I said.

"Yes. One we hired. We sort of inherited Buck with the location. But there's a man named Dex that's worked with us for a long time. He'll be perfect."

"Good. I think that's a smart plan. Even if it's mostly for peace of mind."

She nodded. "That's exactly what I need too, peace of mind." She smiled again. "How about we go join Birdie and Zinnia for a glass of wine? I think we've both earned that. And I promise to practice more tomorrow."

"Sounds good to me. But I might have a Dr Pepper instead."

She laughed and hooked her arm through mine. "I'm sorry you and Sin are leaving in a few days. It's so nice to have you here. Nice to have the cats around too. They're such good company."

"They are. And I'm sorry we have to go, too. But it's our job now." I shook my head. "I can't believe I'm saying this, but it's a lot of fun traveling in that coach. And I am not a girl who likes camping."

"Me either," she said. "And not just because the last thing anyone wants to see is a zombie walking through the woods toward them."

I laughed as we strolled into the kitchen. "I hadn't thought about that."

She waved her fingers at Anson. He was wiping down the counters. "We'd like a glass of pinot noir and a Dr Pepper on the deck."

He snorted. "Oh, I see how it is."

"Well," she said, her tone light and playful. "I'm in recovery. And wine is very restful. Come on, Jayne. Let's go wait for our beverages."

I shot Sin an amused look. And not just because he was up to his elbows in suds at the kitchen sink. I wiggled my index finger at him as we walked away. "That's very sexy, by the way."

He rolled his eyes, smirked at me, and went back to his chores.

It really was sexy. Which was a little surprising. Who knew a man washing dishes in a T-shirt and jeans could be so hot? Or maybe the hotness came from him already being my husband and already being pretty smoking. Whatever the reason, it reminded me what a lucky, lucky girl I was.

Lila and I went outside, and I was a little surprised to see Spider and Sugar out there, lounging on the deck. They had their collars on, but there was nothing to keep them from wandering. No leashes, no fence. Just the pool and then wide-open yard beyond that.

"Spider," I said. "What are you doing out here?"

He barely glanced over his shoulder at me. "Spider knows, Mama. No running off."

Well, at least he remembered that. Although

he was starting to remind me of a slightly petulant teenager.

Sugar looked at me, too. "We know, Momlady. No running off."

"Good. You'd better not." I hoped they really understood that. Maybe a little extra deterrent would help. "Or coyotes might eat you."

Sugar sat up. "Coyote?"

I sat next to Birdie. "It's like a wild dog."

A rather concerned expression took over Sugar's furry white face. "Sugar don't like that."

Birdie snorted, then lightly slapped my arm. "You're scaring the babies. Stop that." She shook her head. "Don't worry, Sugar, honey. No coyotes will come around here as long as they smell wolf. Aunt Birdie will protect you."

Sugar walked over to Birdie, jumped up on her lap, and stared me down as she settled in. "Sugar like Aunt Birdie."

"Yeah, yeah," I said.

Birdie laughed as she petted Sugar. "That's what you get for being a meanie."

Before I could protest, Anson came out with our drinks. "Is the kitchen help allowed to join you when our chores are done?"

Zinnia held up her nearly empty glass. "Only after refills."

He laughed. "Okay, on it."

In a few minutes and after a round of refills,

the men joined us. Sin sat on the deck by my feet, leaning back against my chair. He, Anson, and Jack all brought beers out with them.

The sky was turning the most amazing colors thanks to the setting sun, and the air had the loveliest hint of coolness to it without a trace of humidity.

"This is nice," Anson said. "We never get to do this because of the show every night. But it's really beautiful out here this time of the evening."

"It is," Lila said. She'd given him her chair only to settle in his lap. He had one arm around her, and I was glad things had resolved with such a happy ending. They were a remarkable couple. A lot like my parents in many ways.

Lila looked at him. "Doesn't mean I won't be happy to get back to work tomorrow."

Jack was standing behind Birdie, one hand on her shoulder. She reached up and laid her hand over his. "We're going to head out in the morning. Off to see the Grand Canyon, then one more overnight before we fly home."

"By plane," Jack said. "Just in case you were wondering."

We all laughed.

I reached over to rest my hand on Birdie's arm. "I'm so glad you were both here. You're the best, Birdie. You really are."

"Happy to help, Princess. How long are you two staying?"

I sighed. "My dad texted earlier to say he'd call in the morning with our next destination, so I imagine we'll be leaving tomorrow too."

Lila's smile grew a little sadder. "It's going to be quiet around here without all of you."

"About that," Zinnia said. "I've decided Canyon Meadows is too boring for me to keep living there. I'm going to move."

Lila perked up. "Are you going to take the guest house like we offered?"

Zinnia shrugged. "That depends."

"On what?" Anson said.

"I want us to have a family meal at least once a week."

Lila nodded. "We can absolutely do that. Anything else?"

Zinnia's mouth set with new determination. "I want a cat."

Anson and Lila both smiled and looked at each other. Anson nodded. "I don't see a problem with that."

"All right then," Zinnia said. "I'll move in."

Sin sat up a little. "That's great, Aunt Z. How long will it take you to sell your place at Canyon Meadows, do you think?"

She gave him a sly look. "It sold last week."

He chuckled. "Then maybe I should be asking how long it'll take to get the moving trucks here."

"Thursday," she answered without a beat. "And

I have an appointment to adopt at least one cat at a local rescue the following Saturday."

"Hold on," Anson said. "At least *one* cat? That's not what you said a second ago."

"Don't try me, Anson." Zinnia arched her brows. "The more you fuss, the more cats I will bring home."

As we all laughed, I savored the happiness of the moment and gazed at my husband in complete admiration. Not only had I married well, because Sin was such an amazing guy, but how incredible was it to end up with a family like his to boot? They were wonderful, welcoming people.

Getting Lila home would forever be one of the great accomplishments of my life. My heart was full, my soul was light, and I'd never been more in love.

I'd also never been more curious as to where our next adventure would take us.

Thanks for reading!

Want to be up to date on new books, audiobooks & other fun stuff from Kristen Painter? Sign-up for my newsletter on my website. No spam, just news (sales, freebies, releases, you know, all that jazz.)

www.kristenpainter.com

If you loved the book and want to help the series grow, tell a friend about the book and take time to leave a review!

Other Books by Kristen Painter

COZY MYSTERY:

Jayne Frost series:
Miss Frost Solves a Cold Case: A Nocturne Falls Mystery
Miss Frost Ices the Imp: A Nocturne Falls Mystery
Miss Frost Saves the Sandman: A Nocturne Falls Mystery
Miss Frost Cracks a Caper: A Nocturne Falls Mystery
When Birdie Babysat Spider: A Jayne Frost Short
Miss Frost Braves the Blizzard: A Nocturne Falls Mystery
Miss Frost Chills the Cheater: A Nocturne Falls Mystery
Miss Frost Says I Do: A Nocturne Falls Mystery

Happily Everlasting Series:
Witchful Thinking

PARANORMAL WOMEN'S FICTION:
First Fangs Club series:
Sucks to Be Me
Suck it up, Buttercup
Sucker Punch

PARANORMAL ROMANCE:
Nocturne Falls series:
The Vampire's Mail Order Bride

The Werewolf Meets His Match

The Gargoyle Gets His Girl

The Professor Woos the Witch

The Witch's Halloween Hero – short story

The Werewolf's Christmas Wish – short story

The Vampire's Fake Fiancée

The Vampire's Valentine Surprise – short story

The Shifter Romances the Writer

The Vampire's True Love Trials – short story

The Vampire's Accidental Wife

The Reaper Rescues the Genie

The Detective Wins the Witch

The Vampire's Priceless Treasure

Shadowvale series:
The Trouble With Witches

The Vampire's Cursed Kiss

The Forgettable Miss French

Moody and The Beast

Sin City Collectors series:
Queen of Hearts

Dead Man's Hand

Double or Nothing

Standalone Paranormal Romance:
Dark Kiss of the Reaper

Heart of Fire

Recipe for Magic

Miss Bramble and the Leviathan

URBAN FANTASY:

The House of Comarré series:

Forbidden Blood

Blood Rights

Flesh and Blood

Bad Blood

Out for Blood

Last Blood

The Crescent City series:

House of the Rising Sun

City of Eternal Night

Garden of Dreams and Desires

Nothing is completed without an amazing team.

Many thanks to:

Cover design: MiblArt

Interior formatting: Author E.M.S

Editor/copyedits/proofs: Chris Kridler

About the Author

USA Today Best Selling Author **Kristen Painter** is a little obsessed with cats, books, chocolate, and shoes. It's a healthy mix. She loves to entertain her readers with interesting twists and unforgettable characters. She currently writes two best-selling paranormal romance series: Nocturne Falls and Shadowvale. She also writes the spin off cozy mystery series, Jayne Frost. The former college English teacher can often be found all over social media where she loves to interact with readers:

www.kristenpainter.com

35126880R00169